Charles F. Morse

Letters Written During the Civil War, 1861-1865

Charles F. Morse

Letters Written During the Civil War, 1861-1865

ISBN/EAN: 9783337412074

Printed in Europe, USA, Canada, Australia, Japan

Cover: Foto ©Andreas Hilbeck / pixelio.de

More available books at **www.hansebooks.com**

LETTERS

WRITTEN DURING THE CIVIL WAR

1861 – 1865

PRIVATELY PRINTED

1898

SINE
LABORE
NIHIL

T. R. MARVIN & SON
BOSTON
MASS.
PRINTERS
ESTABL.
1822

TO THE MEMORY

OF

MY MOTHER

NOTE

THE Second Massachusetts Infantry Regiment was organized in April, 1861, immediately after the firing on Fort Sumter.

Colonel George H. Gordon, Lieutenant-Colonel George L. Andrews and Major Wilder Dwight were the active spirits in creating the organization and in securing the acceptance of the regiment by the Secretary of War prior to the first call for troops by President Lincoln, May 4, 1861.

The regiment was mustered into the military service of the United States in the month of May, 1861, at Camp Andrew, West Roxbury It remained at this camp for drill and instruction about two months, and left Boston for the seat of War in Virginia, July 8, 1861.

These letters, written to members of my family, record my experiences as an officer of this regiment during its term of service, from May, 1861, to July, 1865.

CHARLES F. MORSE.

LETTERS

HAGERSTOWN, MD., July 11, 1861.

WE have just arrived here, two o'clock A. M., and have quartered our men in two churches.

I am perfectly well and will write again as soon as I have an opportunity; now, I must get some sleep, as we start to join General Patterson's army early in the day, about twenty miles from here.

* * *

MARTINSBURG, VA., July 15, 1861, Sunday.

I will try and take time to give you an account of the proceedings up to this time since we left Hagerstown.

We started from the latter place about four o'clock, Thursday afternoon, and marched to Williamsport, a distance of seven miles. The men stood the march very well. We reached the side of the Potomac about 6.30, where we camped for the night; nothing occurred of importance during the night except one of the guard being fired upon just before daylight. The camp was aroused at four o'clock, and the column started very soon after. The fording of the river was a very interesting sight. It was about a quarter of a mile wide and two to three feet deep in that place : the regiment marched through it bravely. keeping in close column. As soon as we got over, everything was put in fighting order, as we were told there was a body of cavalry on the look-out to cut us off. Our company was thrown out as rear guard to look out for the wagons, stragglers, etc. Our march was uninterrupted, however, and we arrived at Martinsburg towards night, after a hard march of fifteen miles with no halt except occasional rests; passing by, on our way, the late battleground, on which I picked up a small dirk which had evidently seen service. I have now got to hurry up, as the Quartermaster has just informed us that we march to-morrow morning at five o'clock, and it is now " tattoo."

Our army here is about twenty thousand strong, and is encamped seven miles from General Johnson's rebel force. I suppose our move to-morrow is towards the enemy, although I don't know it.

We had a rather narrow escape from getting into a trap to-day. Colonel Gordon detailed Captain Curtis and myself, with four picked men from each company, to go with the Quartermaster and four wagons to forage. We started off for a place the Quartermaster had been told of, where there were hay and other things we wanted. We had got within about a mile of the place when we met a white man, who happened to be a Unionist, who told us that instead of going to a place where we would get forage, we were within about fifteen minutes' march of about two hundred rebels. We deployed the men instantly, and then the Captain and Quartermaster started back on another track to see what could be found in another direction. In about five minutes, I had orders to carry the party to a house about a half a mile off, that belonged to an out-and-out secessionist. We surrounded it. made our bargain for hay, pigs, chickens, etc., very much against the owner's will, and started back for camp, where we arrived in due time.

You must not expect to hear from me again for some time, as we are going out of the region of mails. I am in the best of health, and we are having cool, comfortable weather.

⋆ ⋆ ⋆

HARPER'S FERRY, VA., July 23, 1861.

Since my letter from Martinsburg, I have hardly had time to take a pen in my hand, we have been so busy.

We left Martinsburg at the time when we were ordered, and took up our position in the column and commenced our march towards "Bunker Hill," where about six thousand of the rebels were encamped six or seven miles from Martinsburg. It was a sight I never shall forget, to see this great army, covering the roads for miles in each direction, with colors flying and bands playing in nearly every regiment; then, after marching about two hours, to hear cannon firing at the head of the column, telling us plainly that we had come up with some part of the enemy. The firing soon stopped, however, and we learned, in a short time, that the rebels were flying in confusion, and that we had killed two and taken several men and horses prisoners.

Before long, we came up to their camps, and it was a singular sight to see them all deserted while the fires were burning and everything in readiness for dinner. We marched on till near night, when our regiment camped in a beautiful grove on the so-called " Bunker Hill." We lay down on the ground that night, as our wagons hadn't come up. However, we were undisturbed and got a good night's rest. The next day, the whole army was allowed to rest, which was needed very much; the only thing that troubled us officers was, that we could get nothing to speak of to eat; we fairly envied the soldiers as they ate their rations. The only way we got along was by begging some coffee and hard bread of the men. At night came the order to have everything ready to start at a moment's notice, and to see that every man was supplied with forty rounds of cartridges and caps. Soon after, Colonel Gordon sent for us to say that, in all probability, we were to move on and attack General Johnston and his army of about twenty-six thousand men, in a very few hours.

The men slept with their rifles in their hands, and we with our swords buckled on, but we were not roused until three o'clock, when "reveille" was sounded in the various camps and, in a short time, we were marching again; but, to our surprise and, I must say, disappointment, we found that we were making what is called a flank movement instead of an advance. Towards afternoon, our line was threatened by cavalry : our company was ordered out by Brigadier-General Abercrombie to act as skirmishers. The enemy, however, kept out of the way, and we soon returned to our position in column. About dark, we halted by the side of a wheat field, and the men were allowed to stack arms and rest, which they needed very much. Captain Curtis and I had just got fast asleep for the night on a pile of wheat, when I was aroused by the Sergeant-Major to be told that I must get ready to go on guard immediately; very disagreeable, of course, but no help for it, so I got up and reported myself for duty. The

Colonel came around before long to caution me about being especially vigilant, as there was a strong chance of an attack. I don't know how I should have got through the night if Major Dwight had not, with his own hands, brought me out some hard-boiled eggs and bread and butter. I devoured them as if I had never eaten anything before. I managed. afterwards, to get some coffee, so I was all right.

The news of our defeat at Bull Run has evidently shaken our General. We are ordered to get ready to move at a moment's notice.

⁂

July 24, Wednesday.

A moment after I stopped writing, I was busy ordering tents struck, wagons packed, and everything got ready for a start. We were almost prepared to move, when General Patterson got a dispatch from General Scott ordering him to stay where he was; so unpack wagons, pitch tents, was the order. We were generally glad of it, as it would have looked as if it were a regular runaway, and we haven't got over feeling sore at not getting to Winchester and giving General Johnston a try.

* * * * * * * * * *

My story left off at Charlestown, where we were last Thursday. About noon, our regiment received orders to march at half-past three P M., on detached service. Everything was moving at the appointed time. We marched out in good spirits, but with empty stomachs. After traveling about a mile, we were informed that we were going to Harper's Ferry to hold the place. I was assigned the honorable command of the rear guard. We had a very pleasant march of eight miles through some of the finest scenery I ever saw. We met with quite a reception in the town; men, women and children cheering us, waving flags, and evidently overjoyed to see United States troops again. We camped on a high bluff just over the Potomac, and proceeded to put the town in a state of martial law, taking several leading secessionists prisoners. Here we got plenty to eat; my first purchase was a gallon of milk; Captain Curtis and myself drank the whole of it before we lay down for the night. The next day we had a good rest. Captain Curtis picked up, during the day, information of a party of troopers that were camped over the other side of the Shenandoah, and obtained permission to take me and forty men and find them, if we could, that night. We called our men out at twelve and started. It was very dark, and there was a severe thunderstorm. We were ferried across the Shenandoah, and scouted all over the mountains, visiting every farm-house and barn, but we found we were just too late, as they had left, suspecting our approach. We got back to camp at eight or nine o'clock, wet and tired, having traveled some ten miles over the roughest possible roads.

❧ ❧ ❧

HARPER'S FERRY, July 26, 1861.

Reveille roll-call is just finished, and I have a short time before breakfast to improve by writing. We still garrison the town, and very hard work it is, too, it taking five companies a day to do it, making guard duty come every other day. What we principally have to do is to keep the rum-shops closed to the soldiers. At night we have patrols on the streets all about the town, and any one found out after nine P M. is sent to his house or quarters, or if suspicious-looking. taken to the guard-room, which, by the way, is the very engine house where John Brown made his final stand. The loop-holes and all are just as he left them.

We also guard all the ferries very carefully. The other night. when I was on guard, there was a report brought to me of a fight in a house a little ways off. I took a Sergeant and eight men and went. double quick, to the place ; the house was full of men, fighting and drunk. We cleared it in about two minutes. took the noisiest, prisoners, then went back and emptied a rum barrel that had caused the whole of it. Such things were occurring frequently, two or three days ago, but. as the Pennsylvania militia go home, we have less and less of it. They are going home at the rate of two regi-ments a day, and we are glad of it, for a more undisciplined set of men I never saw, spoiling everything they come near, breaking into houses. robbing. orchards. and doing all manner of harm generally. Our force will be about eight thousand, when they are all gone. General Banks arrived here, night before last. with two or three of his aides. We all hope he will do something more for us than Patterson has. You can form no idea of the terrible destruction of government build-ings here. without seeing it. For nearly half a mile along the river were these splendid works, and now there is nothing but bare walls and heaps of ruins ; they say twelve million dollars will not replace them. All the bridges across the Potomac and Shenandoah are also burned.

HARPER'S FERRY, VA., July 30, 1861.

Our regiment is now left here alone, the whole army having moved across the Potomac together with all our baggage-
wagons. We are quartered in some of the least ruined government buildings; our picket guards extend some two miles
out into the country around.

There was quite an excitement here the night we first
raised the American flag on the staff at the Arsenal. There
was a large fragment of the secession flag flying at the head
of it when we arrived in town, but it was so securely fastened
that it could not be taken down without a person's climbing
to the top. As the staff was one hundred and five feet high,
this was quite an undertaking. Several tried, but had to
give it up. Finally, our First Sergeant secured fresh hal-
yards and raised the Stars and Stripes. Half the town had
gathered together in the yard, together with a great part of
our regiment. As our flag was run up, the band struck up
"Yankee Doodle," following with the "Star Spangled Ban-
ner." The excitement was, for this latitude, immense.

Those who have been abroad say that this town reminds
them strongly of foreign towns by its narrow, dark streets,
dirty, steep alley-ways, peculiar stone houses, etc. Our mess
chests have been extremely useful to us. Wherever we
could get at our wagons, we have used them entirely to get
our meals with and to eat from, our servants managing the
cooking of chickens, mutton chops, tea, coffee, etc., very well.
Our mess consists of Captain Curtis, Captain Mudge, Bob
Shaw, Tom Robeson and myself; we have very good times
whenever we can all get together, which is not very often,
there being so much special service.

MARYLAND HEIGHTS, July 31, 1861.

It is just about midnight; I am seated in the guard tent and have just finished my guard report; as I have to keep awake all night, I cannot spend my time better than by writing home.

After closing my letter of the 29th, all but Companies A, G, and C were ordered across the river to take position on an elevated plateau as guard to the Rhode Island Battery which commands the ford and ferry. We forded the Potomac in the middle of the afternoon, and climbed up a steep, rough road to our new camping ground, an elevation of some six or seven hundred feet above the river. Rifles were stacked and knapsacks unslung in time for the men to get the fires going and coffee boiling at the usual time, as well as the few preparations necessary for bivouacking. In the mean time, our own stomachs craved a little food. Luckily for our mess, Bob Shaw had been with the pioneer guard that came up with the Rhode Island Battery, and had spotted a very neat little log farm house quite near our camp, and engaged suppers for us. We found a very neat-looking hostess with the romantic name of Buckles, waiting tea for us. She had some nice broiled chickens, apple sauce, bread and molasses, etc., set up in tempting array on a clean white cloth, and altogether, we had the most Christian-like meal, I think, since we left home. We made arrangements for our board while we staid here, and have been living there ever since.

About five minutes after we had lain down for the night, who should come along but C. Wheaton, Adjutant, with an order saying that Company B was detailed for picket guard, to extend from camp down to the main road and canal, and to guard the ferry and ford, and to give a sudden alarm if our three companies the other side of the river were attacked. Nothing could have been more agreeable to us, and the men, of course, were delighted to jump up, with their wet boots and tired legs, after the hard afternoon's march, to have the pleasure of going on twelve hours' more duty! But orders are orders, and in less than fifteen minutes, we were moving down our break-neck path full of rolling stone, and dark as a pocket. Our guard was soon posted; we had a quiet night and were relieved at daybreak. Our breakfast was eaten with a relish, and two or three hours' sleep set us up all right. As I said in my last letter, we have got used to everything now, and when, by chance, we get a six hours' sleep on a stretch, it is considered a luxury worth taking note of.

*   *   *

MARYLAND HEIGHTS, August 5, 1861.

We still are in the same place my last letter was dated from, but instead of being in tents, we are bivouacking again. Last Thursday afternoon, the order came that, as we were the advance guard, we should not have our wagons and baggage liable to being cut off. Everything was moved off in a hurry, and the men set to work building shelters of bushes.

They are built like long sheds, have posts every little distance, rafters and string pieces connecting them. For the reason that we have two architects at the head of our company, ours was the soonest and best built. Captain Curtis and I had an elegant little bower made for ourselves where we live cool and comfortable.

MARYLAND HEIGHTS, August 11, 1861.

There is nothing very new to write, everything is quiet; drills go on three times daily. I had command of the picket at Sandy Hook Thursday night, consisting of some sixty men. We had frequent alarms, through the night, from the other side of the river, caused by firing across the Shenandoah; the long roll was beaten and several of the battalions turned out under arms, but nothing came of it but a pig and dog being killed on our side. The orders to me were to allow no one to pass the ford or ferry without a pass from General Banks or Colonel Gordon, and to shoot any one who attempted to pass without.

I had an interview with Banks Friday morning, to get some orders from him, and give him some information. He was very pleasant and gave me a great deal of discretionary power about shutting up stores, hotels, etc., whenever I had any trouble with liquor. The whole discipline of the army is improving very fast; the soldiers and officers are all obliged to stay by their camps except on special occasions. There is going to be an examination before a military board of officers which will probably throw out a great many inefficient ones. I am happy to say we get some of our pay very soon now; our muster rolls have gone to Washington, and the Paymaster will be here some time this week. We are paid from May 11th until June 30th, this time; that is for me about one hundred and forty dollars.

I just heard that we were to move away from here to-morrow and join our brigade, some four miles off. I shall be glad, on some accounts, as it will join our regiment together again and get us off from this continual guard duty. The weather here is steadily hot, averaging from ninety to one hundred degrees.

✲ ✲ ✲

Monday, August 12, 1861.

We have just got back with our company from Battery Hill, where we have been on guard. It rained, pouring, all night; our rubber blankets were our only protection. We got pretty wet, but I have just had a good, hot breakfast and feel very comfortable; the only thing is, we have no dry camp to go to. We are going to fortify our position, and the word is now that we are to hold this place until we are driven out. We have lost our Quartermaster; he has accepted a position as aide on General Banks' staff; probably Motley will be appointed in his place. The Chaplain goes down with the letters shortly, so I must stop.

✲ ✲ ✲

JEFFERSON, MD., August 22, 1861.

I dare say you are surprised to see where we are, and at not having heard from me for some time, but I have had no time to write, on account of various movements, expeditions, being without tents and wagons, etc. I shall give you, as soon as we are in camp again, a journal of what we've been doing for the last ten days. Yesterday, after shifting around for about a week since the army moved, we received orders to march and join our brigade. Just think, we have been on detached service for a month: the only regiment out of this army that has had anything of the kind to do!

BUCKEYSTON, MD., August 23, 1861.

Before starting on our march again, I am going to try and take time to write you some account of what is going on, and of what has happened the last week; as I have kept a journal of it, I will give it to you according to that.

Thursday, August 15th : —

I was ordered this morning to be ready, immediately after breakfast, with the company armed with picks, shovels, axes and bars, to proceed to join two other companies and work on a road that was building across the mountain. Captain Curtis did not go, as the road was in charge of another Captain.

Friday, August 16th : —

Working on the road the same as yesterday until about five o'clock P M., when an orderly came to me with an order to report at camp immediately; arrived there and found everything getting ready for a start. At eight o'clock, the order "fall in," was given, and we were soon on our way down the mountain; a dark night and pouring rain. On arriving down at the foot of the mountain, we were strung along by companies between there and Sandy Hook. We then learned that the whole army had moved to Point of Rocks to cut off a rebel force that was said to be marching on Baltimore. The night was uncomfortable on account of the rain and having to bunk down on the road without blankets, but we managed to get through it.

Saturday, August 17th : —

Nothing in particular done until afternoon, when Companies B, D, I and E were sent across to Harper's Ferry under Lieutenant-Colonel Andrews to seize some flour. We took possession of all the roads leading to the town, built barricades, etc., and held them through the night while seven hundred and eighty barrels of flour were carried across the river. Another rainy, cold night.

Sunday, August 18th : —

Back to Sandy Hook. I managed this morning to get a few hours' sleep to make up for the last two nights; it refreshed me very much. In the afternoon, we marched two miles further on, leaving two companies to guard the ford and ferry. On halting, we found six of our wagons with our tents, which were immediately pitched. At night, the companies at the river were relieved; we then heard that there had been a little skirmish after we had left. Some three hundred cavalry had scoured into town and begun firing at our men; this was quickly returned, and resulted in the enemy losing three or four wounded, which disconcerted them and they left.

Monday, August 19th : —

In the afternoon, we were ordered to the ferry with our company to keep guard for twenty-four hours. We had frequent alarms, but nothing of any consequence happened.

Tuesday, August 20th : —

We were relieved at six o'clock P M., by Company A, and learned from them that the regiment was being paid off. We got our pay-rolls signed that night, and (Aug. 21st) were paid this morning, each man receiving eighteen dollars and seventy-four cents pay, up to the 30th of June. I got my full pay of one hundred and eight dollars a month, one hundred and eighty-four dollars and forty-five cents. We are paid again in less than a month, when I shall get two hundred and sixteen dollars and ninety cents. It makes me feel quite flush to see so much gold, all 1861 pieces. At twelve o'clock, noon, the regiment started to join our brigade and marched six miles to Jefferson, a very pretty town, where we camped for the night.

August 22d : —

Marched eight miles to Buckeyston, over hard roads on account of the heavy rains. Camped for the night here. I have now arrived up to date, and must stop, as we start soon. I shall send some money home at the very first place I can get hold of Adams Express. I have had but one mail for several days. so I've no doubt there are several letters for me somewhere.

❧ ❧ ❧

HYATTSTOWN, MD., August 26, 1861.

We are finally located with our brigade, which we joined Friday towards night, after marching from Buckeyston about eight miles. Saturday noon a mail arrived containing all our back letters.

* * * * * * * * * *

Our camp here is quite a nice one. Most of General Banks' army is right about in the vicinity. Directly about us there are some twelve thousand men. The nearest rebel camp is about fifteen miles off, over the river at Leesburg, where there are nearly thirty thousand of the enemy. I am writing this in my guard tent. It is nearly one o'clock A. M., and I have just sent a corporal to wake Captain Coggswell who is "officer of the day," that he may make the "grand rounds." The camp is perfectly quiet; my candle and one in the hospital tent are the only lights to be seen anywhere.

The silence is broken only by the snoring of the first and third reliefs, who are "off," and by the footsteps of the second relief, who are "on." I hear now, in the distance, the sentry challenge: "Who goes there?" "Grand rounds!" "Halt, grand rounds!" "Advance Sergeant with the countersign." "The countersign is right; advance, rounds!"

Captain C. has been and gone; he reports everything correct. There is no excitement now until "reveille," at five. Captain Mudge and company started for Washington yesterday morning as guard to a wagon train. Washington is about thirty miles off; I should not be much surprised if we all got there before long.

It is now two o'clock and I must inspect a relief, so I'll close up this interesting epistle and put on my sword which I've taken off, contrary to regulations, and step out into the moonlight.

❧ ❧ ❧

PLEASANT HILL, MD., Sept. 1, 1861.

Since writing my last letter, we (General Banks' division) have moved some fourteen miles, so that we are now within twenty miles of Washington; you need not be surprised if my next letter comes from the latter place, although we know nothing at all of our movements until we get marching orders. These are given us, say, at nine o'clock at night. "Reveille" is ordered to be at four A. M., and the cooks are directed to cook a day's rations. At four, everybody is tumbled up, men get their breakfasts, pack their knapsacks, and have their day's rations served out and put in their haversacks. At six, the "general" is sounded, and at the last roll of the drum, every tent comes down as if by magic. It is the greatest change you can imagine; one minute you see the field covered with these great Sibley tents, the next nothing but a mob, apparently, of men. By seven, the wagons are packed, the line formed, we wheel into columns, regiment joins brigade, brigade joins division, the column is formed and we start.

By the way, I never told you anything about "our" brigade. It is the '*Second*,' under command of Colonel Abercrombie, an old army officer who has seen a great deal of service; it consists of the Second and Twelfth Massachusetts and the Twelfth and Sixteenth Indiana regiments. We have the right of the line. We are camped now on the top of a hill close by General Banks' headquarters; the rest of the brigade is in the same field with us; on the other side of the road are two or three other regiments, and several more within sight. At night it looks like a great city; every tent is illuminated and hundreds of camp-fires are all about us. It is a fine sight. Then, too, there is continual music from the various bands which play until " tattoo " stops them.

Our last march from Hyattstown was through a pouring rain all day and any quantity of mud. To top off with, we had no tents for the night. You would have thought that if ever men might grumble, it was then. I did not hear one of our company open his mouth to complain, although they, as well as we, had to lie down on the ground without any hot suppers. Camp-fires of rail fences were a comfort that night. I got along very well by taking two fence rails, laying them parallel and filling the space between them with straw. Towards morning, the fire got low, and I had to burn my bedstead to keep it from going out.

You know I said something in my last letter about the baggage being reduced. The Brigade Quartermaster made us a call yesterday and cut off our mess chests and the Captain's bedstead. We do not lose them; they are being taken to Frederick and receipts given for them. In case of our being in barracks this winter, we shall have them again. We saved our tea, coffee, tea-kettle and our little coffee machine which is worth its weight in gold. The people at the north, I think, have no idea what a fine army ours is becoming under McClellan's influence. The men are being thoroughly drilled and they, as well as the officers, are kept under the strictest discipline. Everybody here is getting confident and longing for the next great event, which must take place before long. We are now within a day's march of Washington, so that, in case of an advance, our chance is good of sharing it.

⚜ ⚜ ⚜

September 18, 1861.

I had the pleasantest time, yesterday, that I have had this long while. General Lander's Brigade, including the Twentieth Regiment, Massachusetts Volunteers, was on the march from Washington to Poolsville; they were to pass within about two miles of our camp, so Captain Curtis and I got permission to go off and see them. It was the first time I had left camp except for picket or other duty, since I left Camp Andrew; it seemed very much of a holiday. We met the Twentieth after about three-quarters of an hour's march. I tell you we were glad to see so many good fellows; at least a dozen of them were intimate friends; Charley Pierson, the Adjutant, Bill Bartlett, Caspar Crowninshield, John Putnam,

Harry Tremlett, and lots of others. They were all looking well, dusty and sunburnt. Captain Schmidt seemed very glad to see me; he was very unchanged. After walking a mile or two with them, we returned to camp well pleased with our visit. Poolsville, where they are now encamped, is seven miles from us.

I have just made me a delicious cup of black coffee; it will keep me awake the rest of the night, I think, as it is now near one. I have been on court-martial for the last two or three days; Rufus Choate was Judge Advocate. The way we put cases through would have astonished a police court.

Captain Curtis went on to Washington, to-night, to rectify an error in the date of pay roll: he will be back some time to-morrow or next day. General McClellan is going to review General Banks' division Tuesday. It will be a great sight, if they can find a good place for it; fifteen thousand troops marching company front. Ellis has been made brigade commissary, a regular staff appointment. Sedgwick has received an appointment on some staff with the rank of major. Lieutenant Howard and Tom Robeson have been made signal officers, and are detached. Copeland has gone on to Banks' staff, and there is some talk of making Charley Horton or Steve Perkins ordnance officers of this division, so you see our roster of officers is quite reduced. If anybody is wanted for any purpose in this division, our regiment is sure to be called on to supply him: it is complimentary to us, to be sure, but it makes it rather hard for the rest. You asked me, in a letter some time ago, if I was trying to get a commission in the regular army. Not a bit of it' I shall try for one some of these days, likely, but not till I have seen some service. I should not care for anything less than a captaincy in the regular army, and it will be a good while before I can expect that. I suppose you notice by my talk that I don't think we have a short war before us; the more I think of it, the more I think it will be a long one. I saw a list of Tom Stevenson's officers, the other day. There are several very good companies, Bob Clark's, Bob Steve's and some others.

Captain Robert Williams, General Banks' Assistant Adjutant-General, has got a furlough from the regular army, and is going to take command of the cavalry regiment now raising in Massachusetts; rather singular that he, a Virginian, should be the Colonel of a regiment raised to fight his own State. He is a very fine officer, and I should think would be much liked; his present rank is that of captain.

You will hardly believe it when I tell you that the men of our regiment look better now as regards their rifles, accoutrements and dress, than they did at Camp Andrew. At dress parades and inspections, we insist on every man having his shoes and belts shining bright with blacking, also on every button and bit of brass about their firelock being polished, and, if on drawing the rammer from the barrel, there is enough rust or dirt on it to soil a white glove, the man who owns it is obliged to clean it (the rifle), immediately after parade, to the satisfaction of his officer. Their clothes are considerably worn, but the general effect is far better than ever before. We have earned the name of the "stuck up" Massachusetts Regiment, which amuses us considerably. Others think we cannot get along well with our men, as they never see them sitting around in our tents smoking and joking with us and enjoying themselves generally, as they are allowed to do in some regiments. We let them think so.

CAMP NEAR CONRAD'S FERRY, MD.,
October 24, 1861.

My last letter left off rather abruptly, and as a series of exciting events has taken place since then, I will try and detail them nearly as they occurred. I left off just as Captain Curtis got back from Banks' headquarters with the good news that we were to join our regiment and march at once towards the river.* We didn't stop to strike tents or pack the wagons, but left a small squad of weak men to do it. We packed our trunks and other traps and piled them up together in our tent. At half past eight P M., the regiment marched by so quietly that one would not have known that there were more than ten men on the road; no drum or any other music. At nine, our company was ready and started. Before we were off, we could see, by the camp fires, that the whole division had marching orders. Going at quickest time, we caught the regiment at a halt; the night was cloudy, but the moon made it quite light. At twelve thirty we got to Poolsville, distance ten miles; here we began to hear rumors of the fight; men on guard told us that the Fifteenth Massachusetts and several other regiments had been cut to pieces in crossing the river near Conrad's Ferry; one said the Ffteenth had lost seven hundred men; we disbelieved them almost entirely.

As we got nearer to the river, the stories began to get more probable, and when within two or three miles of it, to confirm them, we met numbers of wounded who said that the Twentieth and Fifteenth Massachusetts and the California

---

* Company B had been on detached service as Provost guard for about ten days.

and Tammany regiments were in the fight and were all more or less cut up. At about five A. M., we reached the river, distance twenty-one miles from the camp, a splendid march, made with very few halts, the men all carrying their knapsacks.

Here, as daylight came on, we began to hear the terrible truth; the houses all about us were filled with dead and wounded, and down the river about a mile, there was a temporary hospital with over a hundred men in it. Of course, my first inquiries were for my friends in the Twentieth; I could hear nothing definite. Shortly afterwards, Captain Curtis received a message from Lieutenant Willie Putnam, a splendid young fellow, saying he would like to see him. From the Major, Captain C. and others, I learned, when they came back, the following: That Colonel Lee and Major and Doctor Revere were prisoners and probably carried to Leesburgh; that Lieutenant W Putnam was mortally wounded by a shot through the body; Captain C. saw him and said he conversed as calmly about the events of the battle as if he had been a spectator instead of an actor; he said the wound was quite painful, but by his face you would not have known it. (He died this morning.) Captain John Putnam had his arm taken off close to the shoulder by a round shot; he was brought across the river and is in the hospital. Captain Crowninshield had just swam across the river; he had fought splendidly, others say, all through the battle, had been unable to retreat with the rest, and had hid over night. He was unhurt. Poor young Holmes was badly shot through the body and arm; he and Lieutenant Lowell saw Charley Peirson, the Adjutant, fall, and ran up to attempt to bring him off; as they lifted him from the ground, they were all three shot down, Lowell through the leg. Holmes is likely to recover, Lowell is doing well, Peirson is a prisoner. George Perry is missing. Harry Sturgis, Harry Tremlett and Charley Whittier, got off safely. All of these that I have mentioned were down at Fort Independence in the Guards, and Putnam, Peirson and Tremlett were in the same mess with me. Captain Schmidt, I believe, is badly shot through the body. I am not certain about it.

My understanding of the affair is this : — Brigadier-General Baker was ordered by Brigadier-General Stone to take a certain number of regiments and cross the river at Conrad's Ferry. while he, Stone, was crossing at Edward's Ferry, five miles below, with his force. The troops were all landed on an island first, I believe ; their only means of conveyance was one flat boat. Four companies of the Fifteenth crossed first, and, without waiting for reinforcements, foolishly moved forward towards Leesburgh. of course stirring up the enemy's pickets and alarming the country.

Parts of the Twentieth, Fifteenth, California and New York regiments now followed, making the whole force over the river about fifteen or eighteen hundred men and two guns. The fight, at first, was skirmishing almost entirely, the enemy being out of sight in the woods ; their firing was very heavy, and it was evident, from the first, that they had numbers of sharpshooters lodged in the trees and everywhere else, to pick off the officers. Those who were there say that the Massachusetts men fought splendidly, making no confusion, and falling back perfectly orderly to the river, which they were fairly driven into, numbers drowning, others swimming to the island and Maryland shore. Of course, the great mistake of the whole affair was trying to cross an unfordable river with an insufficient force, unsupported by artillery and with no means of retreat; any one of these things would almost be sure to cause defeat. It is almost fortunate that General Baker was killed, as he would have been constantly reproached by everybody and could have hardly kept his commission. How much General Stone was to blame, no one can yet say; his orders to Baker were to cross in a discreet manner.

About the detail of the loss of the Fifteenth, I cannot say, as I know no one in it. The Colonel of it told Mr. Quint last night that he had lost near half of his regiment and twelve of his commissioned officers. The Lieutenant-Colonel lost his leg. To go back to our regiment. We were left along between the canal and the river. Early in the morning, it commenced to rain, pouring, and continued till night; we had nothing but mud to stand in and were wet and uncomfortable. At about ten A. M., I was detailed by Colonel Gordon to take a dozen good men and get a small flat boat there was up the river, and cross with it to the island to bring off a number of our men who were beckoning for aid from there. We got the boat and crossed successfully. The men were from different regiments and had hidden over night; they were very glad of the chance to get back into a friendly State. Not a Secesher made his appearance. The current was strong but the water was not very deep.

Towards night, our regiment moved a little ways back into the woods, where we pitched tents, built fires, got dry, and changed stockings, besides getting something to eat for a change. Next morning, we changed camp, moving back about two miles to get out of reach of the enemy's shells. Five of our companies were out on picket the whole of the night before, in all the rain, without fires. On arriving in

camp, our company was put on guard. Just before supper
time, I saw a mounted officer ride fast into camp and go up
to a group where Lieutenant-Colonel Andrews was standing,
and whisper something to him. Two minutes afterwards, I
received an order to have the "general" beaten, which is the
signal for every man to be at his quarters and strike tents;
twenty minutes afterwards, the "assembly" was beaten, the
line formed and immediately put in motion towards Edward's
Ferry. Although the regiment was jaded, it moved off in
fine shape, every one thinking we were sure of a fight. Getting near the river, we were surprised to see the camp of a
large army about their usual duties, no signs of a movement.
We marched straight to the river and halted for orders. The
first I heard was, "Countermarch by file right, march!"
The Colonel came by and said to Captain Curtis, "Where
do you suppose we are going?" "I don't know." "Back
to camp!" An attack on the other side had been expected
and the order had been sent to us to come on. The alarm
blew over, our orders were countermanded, but by some miserable mistake, were not transmitted. We had marched six
miles for nothing. We started back at ten and got into camp
at twelve.

Our dead on the other side of the river were treated
shamefully; every pocket was slit down and rifled and every
button and shoe taken off. Probably our company goes on
picket to-night at the island; if it does not, I shall go over
to the Twentieth. Just heard that Captain Schmidt got four
balls in his leg and side. He only feels afraid he will not
be able to fight them in the next battle. He is doing well.
You had better direct to General Banks' division via Washington.

CAMP NEAR MUDDY BRANCH,
November 6, 1861.

"Tattoo" roll call is just over and I shall take the interval till bed-time to write you a brief letter.

The mail came in a short time ago, and I received your very pleasant letter of the 2d. I always kept very quiet about Captain Curtis' going away, because I couldn't bear to believe it possible. For two or three months, we have lived in the same tent and have been together constantly, and I think he felt almost as badly when he went away as I did. I shall not think anything about getting a position in the cavalry regiment, as the chances are so small. I know Captain Curtis will do all he can for me. I should like to be a cavalry officer for several reasons. It is the highest grade of the service, and it is more dignified to have two or three horses and ride, than to go on foot; then, after you are well drilled, you are sure of more active service than in infantry.

Lieutenant Williams will undoubtedly have this company, although nothing has yet been done about it. He had the luck to be second on the roll of first lieutenants; I am sixth, so you see my captaincy is in the distance. I have got a fine wood fire burning in a fireplace in my tent; it makes it very comfortable. The weather is very cold, freezing almost every night.

✤ ✤ ✤

November 22, 1861.

I have just passed a very pleasant Thanksgiving, and will give you a little description of it. Yesterday was very pleasant, quite mild for a change. In the morning at ten o'clock,

we had church services. Mr. Quint officiated and read the
Governor's proclamation, music by the band, etc. After this
we officers had a "turkey shoot." Then came dinner for the
men. I provided our company the following: eleven turkeys, seven geese, eighteen chickens, one hundred and forty
pounds of plum pudding. It was all nicely cooked at a farm
house and looked as well as need be. It was quite a feast
and was enjoyed highly. Other companies were treated accordingly. I doubt if most of the men ever had as good a
Thanksgiving before. The turkeys we shot we gave to the
non-commissioned officers. At four thirty, after dress parade,
we had our dinner. The tent was nicely warmed by a fire-
place running under it, and well lighted by candles in fes-
toons. We had very nice stewed and raw oysters to start off
with, followed by roast turkeys, geese. celery, etc. We had
plenty of champagne and plum pudding, and everything
passed off pleasantly. In the midst of the dinner, Lieutenants Grafton and Shelton arrived (very opportunely for
them), and joined us. We sat till near "tattoo," smoking
and singing: then dispersed. The usual supper of cold goose
without mince pie, was eaten about eleven o'clock. Altogether, it was a very pleasant day, much more so than I
anticipated. The band played during dessert, in the ap-
proved style.

Tuesday, Wheaton was taken sick. I have been acting
as Adjutant ever since. I like it very well for a change.

If you see Rufus Choate, tell him about our Thanksgiving; we were very sorry to lose his company on that occasion, he is such a good fellow.

❧   ❧   ❧

CAMP HICKS, NEAR FREDERICK, MD.,
December 8, 1861.

I take the opportunity of Captain Williams' going home to send a letter direct. Last Tuesday morning, about half-past twelve o'clock, I was fast asleep as usual, but was awakened by some one saying, "Mr. Morse." I answered, "What?" and got the following order: "Send a circular around to the commanders of companies, saying that reveille will be beaten at half-past five, the men to be ready to march as soon afterward as possible, with three days' rations." I asked if that came from the Colonel; the answer was, "I'm the Colonel." I begged his pardon and got up, lighted a fire and wrote the circular and sent my orderly round to the captains. Everything was executed as per order, the usual lively scene of striking tents and packing wagons, and by half-past seven, we were ready to start.

It was a very cold, clear day; so cold that, though I had a horse, in my capacity as adjutant, I hardly mounted him all day; we all had to wear overcoats. We marched between seventeen and eighteen miles to the village of Barnsville, arriving there near four o'clock. We pitched tents in a thick wood, and the men were immediately employed getting their dinners and making arrangements for a comfortable night. I got a very nice dinner at General Abercrombie's headquarters, a house in the town. It was an awfully cold night; water froze nearly an inch thick.

Reveille was beaten Wednesday morning at half-past four, and we left our camping ground as soon as there was light enough to see our way through the woods, about half-past six. The weather was so cold that we marched ten miles without a halt, through a very rough, mountainous country. After a short rest, we went on five miles farther through a splendid farming country, a pleasant thing for us to see after the desolate region we had been living in. We camped a short distance from Frederick. The next morning, after a very nice breakfast at a miller's, the regiment marched to its present camp, situated in a wood about three miles from the city. It is a very pleasant place, with a warm southern slope, and is a neat looking camp. We are near enough to the city to get anything we want from it, which is very convenient. I haven't been in yet; several of the officers have, and find it a very pleasant and civilized city.

* * *

CAMP HICKS, MD.. December 16, 1861.

I walked into Frederick yesterday to do some business pertaining to the company and a little for myself. It is rather a pretty city, about the size of Cambridge, with a number of very nice churches and private residences. The streets are full of officers and soldiers, and on the corner of every street, there is a sentinel posted; occasionally a patrol goes through the thoroughfare to seize any drunken soldiers or stop disturbances. However, their duties are light, as the soldiers find it very much for their interest to keep sober and quiet when they have passes. I was glad to get back to camp; if there is anything forlorn, it is to walk about in a city where you know nobody and have nothing particular to do. A camp becomes your whole world, bounded by a line of sentries, when you live in it as much as we have lived in ours. My visit to the city was, I believe, my fourth absence from camp since leaving Camp Andrew.

We had services this morning; Mr. Quint conducted them, as usual. I think it is getting rather cold weather for out-door preaching, and shall not feel very badly for stormy Sundays. The last fortnight has been remarkably pleasant, the weather generally quite warm; the nights are cold. Imagine yourself going out before sunrise and washing your face and hands, with the mercury standing in the thermometer at twelve degrees, as it was here two or three days ago. Captain Tucker's resignation has been accepted and Harry Russell is now assigned to the command of Company H. George Bangs is now first on the list of first lieutenants and I am second.

⁂

CANTONMENT HICKS, February 13, 1862.

The splendid news of the fight and victory of Roanoke Island reached us this morning, and has caused great excitement and enthusiasm. We are most anxious to hear the particulars, especially as the Twenty-fourth is mentioned as being terribly cut up by the fire from the batteries. It will be dreadful to hear of any of our friends being among the killed or wounded. What a record there will be for the New England Guards after the war is over! I believe all its old members have done well so far; after the Second has been heard from, the list will be complete. Our news from the west is scarcely less interesting; what a plucky and successful thing that was for those gun-boats to go right through the heart of Tennessee and into Alabama! It's a great pity they couldn't have stayed to the ball at Florence.

Last night, General Banks received a telegram from General McClellan saying that he, the latter, wanted five hundred men from Banks' division to go out to join the gun-boat expedition down the Mississippi ; they were all to be volunteers. We were called upon to furnish thirty from our regiment, three from a company. As soon as it became known to the men, there was a perfect rush from the company streets to the captains' tents; everybody wanted to go. We chose three good fellows from " B," who when they found out they were the lucky ones, were perfectly wild; one, a fine, big Irishman, that I enlisted at Chicopee, jumped right up in the air and gave a regular wild Irish whoop.

❧ ❧ ❧

CANTONMENT HICKS, February 24, 1862.

Last Friday my two boxes arrived while I was on guard. I had them carried to my tent and invited my friends for Saturday night. Saturday, the 22d, our regiment went into Frederick with the brigade to parade through the streets, so I had a good chance to make my preparations. I borrowed a *white tablecloth* of a civilian, and the necessary dishes from our mess, silver, etc. Everything came out of the boxes in perfect order; the pudding *dish* was broken, but the pudding was all right. I found your note describing the contents, stuck to a pie. Dinner was ordered to be ready at half-past five and at that time punctually my guests made their appearance, hungry as bears after their ten-mile tramp. The table had a truly grand and magnificent appearance. In the centre of the white cloth reposed the turkey in all its glorious proportions, filling the air with its fragrance, its flanks and approaches were well guarded by those noble grouse, currant jelly, potatoes, etc. Plates were set for seven: Captains

Williams and Russell. Lieutenants Shaw, Horton, Perkins, Oakey and myself. Candles suspended over our heads furnished the light in very festive style. Captain Williams carved the turkey in a most scientific manner, it was splendid: if it had not been for the grouse, there would have been very little but bones taken out of the tent, but the grouse, they were perfection; and now I come to *them*, I insist on knowing who sent them; the health of the donor, he or she, was drunk in both Sherry and Madeira, and will be drunk again when the name becomes known. Pudding, pies, coffee and cigars followed in proper order, and after a prolonged sitting of four hours we got up from the table convinced that in future years we should remember the 22d of February, not as Washington's birthday, but as the anniversary of our dinner in Cantonment Hicks. The whole affair was a perfect success, and I am truly thankful to you for the pains and trouble you took to make it so. It will stand out as a bright mark in our usual monotonous routine.

✿ ✿ ✿

HEADQUARTERS CO. B, 2d MASS. REG'T,
CHARLESTOWN, VA., March 2, 1862.

I wrote in my last that we had received marching orders and were liable to be off at any moment. We remained in a state of uncertainty till Wednesday afternoon, when we had the following order: "Reveille at four Thursday morning; march at five; take cars from Frederick at seven."

These orders were complied with on a dark, cloudy, muddy morning, except that we had to wait till half-past seven on the railroad track before we started for Sandy Hook.

Our whole brigade went on this train. After a hard ride of about four hours, we arrived at Sandy Hook. We disembarked as soon as possible, and formed line along the canal. Everything looked as natural as if we had only left the day before, except the lower part of Harper's Ferry, which, you know, Colonel Geary destroyed by burning. We marched down to the ferry, across which there had been a pontoon bridge constructed. We had to cross this in single file to avoid much jarring. It is a beautiful bridge, built in this manner: at intervals of every twenty feet are the pontoons, which look like common flat-bottomed scows, and are connected together by planking about eight feet wide. The whole arrangement is connected to the shore by a system of ropes. The bridge must be at least eight hundred and sixty feet long.

After crossing. we marched through Harper's Ferry, which seemed perfectly full of troops; we went down the Shenandoah road about a mile and quartered the regiment in some empty houses we found. The weather had changed since morning. and the night was very cold, with a perfect gale of wind. Captain Williams, Lieutenant Oakey and myself, found a very good room which we occupied together. At four o'clock next morning, we were awakened by the "officer of the day" ordering us to have our men get their breakfasts. As the regiment was going to move in light marching order at daylight, I got up and hunted for some coffee. I was lucky enough to find one house pretty well supplied, and engaged them to make me ten gallons for our company. We were very fortunate in getting this, as it enabled the men to start off feeling warm and comfortable, which is a great thing.

At seven, our line was formed, and then we learned that we were to form part of a reconnoitering force, to consist of four squadrons of cavalry, four pieces of artillery and two regiments of infantry, the whole under command of Colonel Gordon. As this was a very good specimen of a reconnoissance in force, perhaps you would like to know how it was conducted.

First, a few cavalry skirmishers to scour the roads and fields; then the main body of cavalry; then two pieces of artillery supported by a company of infantry, followed by two more supported similarly; then on each side of the road, a platoon of skirmishers covering near a third of a mile each way; these protect the advance of the main body of infantry: the flanks are protected by skirmishers deployed as flankers. I had the second platoon of our company deployed on the left of the road to drive in any pickets that might be out, or obtain other information; every house we came to, I had a man search from top to bottom, for arms or anything else that might be hidden in them.

Our cavalry skirmishers met those of the enemy just this side of Charlestown, and drove them into their main body; our cavalry then came up at the gallop and sent the enemy flying out of town and a couple of miles into the country, many of them throwing away their arms in their hurry. We followed along and took quiet possession of the town, probably as thoroughly secesh a place as any in Virginia. People scowled at us from their windows, but did not venture much into the streets; those who did seemed almost frightened to death, every one thinking we were going to burn the town. The guns were put in position at once, commanding the Winchester roads. The cry was suddenly set up, " The General is coming!" Ranks were formed and dressed. Presently, Generals McClellan, Banks, and Hamilton, with their staffs and guards, rode by; we saluted, and the General took off his cap to us; he is a splendid looking man, though not much like his pictures. They rode out about two miles and returned. He was so well satisfied with the movement that he decided to have our force remain and occupy the town. Most of our regiment are quartered at the Court House; our company occupies the toll-house of the Charlestown, Berryville and Winchester turnpike, a short distance from the town, supporting a section of Hampton's battery; very comfortable quarters.

We were reinforced, Friday night, by two regiments and a regular battery. That night, our cavalry was several times driven in by the enemy's cavalry: we lost four horses and three men by these attacks, and captured one of the enemy. One of the sentinels of our company shot a cavalry horse through the neck while on picket last night, about a half a mile from our house: the picket fired three times and drove them back.

The only currency here in town is the Southern shinplaster, dreadful mean looking stuff; I will send you a five cent bank bill in a day or two. Coffee costs four dollars a pound here and hard to be had at that. We shall be off from here in a day or two for Winchester, but I do not believe we shall have to fire a gun to take it: then for Richmond via Manassas. This is a little better than sticking in the mud at Frederick. Direct to General Banks' Division, War Department, Washington.

*　*　*

HEADQUARTERS CO. B, BERRYVILLE TOLLHOUSE,
CHARLESTOWN, VA., March 5, 1862.

You see by my elaborate heading that we have not moved since my last letter was written. General Banks has about eight thousand troops in town; General Sedgwick has about ten thousand at Harper's Ferry. I believe that ten or twelve thousand more are to join Banks from Williamsport, what was formerly Lander's division; then, I imagine, all will be ready for an onward movement to Winchester or elsewhere.

I sent, day before yesterday, a few papers I picked up in Andrew Hunter's office. This latter gentleman is some great man in the Confederate Senate; his office is occupied by some of our officers. He was the lawyer employed by the Government in the John Brown case, and those who had the first dip into his legal papers found some very interesting documents; such as a letter from Governor Wise to Mr. Hunter before the trial came on, saying that he had made up his mind not to pardon John Brown or any of his accomplices, but that every one should suffer death. There was another anonymous letter from Boston implicating T. W Higginson, Sanborn and others; also letters from the different prisoners suing for pardon.

Three of our companies are quartered in the Court House; one is in a printing office, from which they have issued various bulletins, such as, " Confederate notes to be had at par; " " Hard bread to be exchanged for chickens; " " Gas wanted by Company D, for the Union Theatre." Our mess has a room formerly occupied by a secesh confectioner: it still retains the smell of peppermint. I drank some rye coffee, the

other day, and liked it very much ; with cream and sugar, it
makes a very good drink. Marching orders! I close for the
present.

♪ ♪ ♪

CAMP NEAR WINCHESTER, March 15, 1862.

I never thought to head a letter as this is headed until
after a hard fight, but so it is. I will give you a short journal of things as they happened to us since I wrote mother
last Sunday.

Monday morning about two thirty, we were again awakened by C. Wheaton, Jr., with the orders, " Wake your cooks ;
cook three days' rations ; reveille at five ; breakfast immediately after ; march at seven."

Reveille and breakfast took place per order, but marching
orders did not arrive until past eleven, when they came post
haste, ordering us to leave tents and baggage and march at
once, as General Gorman, who had gone on with his brigade,
was threatened with an attack. Start we did and marched
eleven miles to Berryville, but saw no enemy. Our brigade
was marched into a wood to bivouac ; we stacked arms in
line of battle and then allowed the men to get straw from
a neighboring stack to make themselves comfortable with.
With the help of rails *borrowed* from fences, various styles of
shelter were rigged up. *We* made one to accommodate four
of us, that was quite comfortable, although the night was
cold and windy, with occasional rain squalls. Hogan and
Tom (Captain Williams' servant), built us a fire, and then
went foraging for a supper ; they succeeded in getting two
or three slices of raw bacon, some hard boiled eggs and a
canteen of milk. With these, we made a good supper, toast-

ing the bacon to a delicate brown and making some good tea
in my faithful tea pot. I have got to be a pretty good cam-
paigner, now, and never start on any kind of a march without
my rubber blanket, my thick woollen one and a haversack
containing a little bag of tea, coffee and sugar, some *hard*
bread, a piece of salt pork and my aforementioned tea and
coffee pot. With these articles, I can make myself and several others happy, no matter where we bring up.

Rolled up in our blankets, with a fire at our feet, we
enjoyed a good night's sleep. The next morning was very
pleasant, although cool ; breakfast was a repetition of supper ;
in fact, almost every meal up to date has been, varying bacon
with pork and tea with coffee. We passed the day lazily ;
four or five regiments and as many batteries came up in the
morning and camped near us. Wednesday was a beautiful,
warm day with us ; our company was detailed for " Grand
Guard."

About five o'clock that afternoon, we received orders to
draw in our vedettes and report with the company at the
camp as soon as possible, as the brigade had received marching orders. We joined the regiment on the Winchester road.
It was a fine, clear moonlight night and we had a very good
road. We marched until nearly half past twelve, to within
a mile of Winchester, and bivouacked in a very thick pine
wood. The trees were so thick that we officers all lost each
other, each one, on finding a comfortable place, settling himself for the rest of the night. I was lucky enough to stumble
across Hogan and got my blanket ; after a good cup of coffee,
I rolled up under a pine tree and slept soundly until morning.
Looking around me at daylight, I saw Captain Williams not
twenty yards from me, alongside of Charley Horton, Captain

Savage and several other officers. George Bangs and Captain Goodwin presented a lamentable appearance, not having brought any blankets. Our wagons came up in good season for the men to get their breakfasts, and at ten, or thereabouts, we pitched our camp in a neighboring field. Yesterday, Bob Shaw and I walked into Winchester to see the sights. It is a rather decayed-looking town, larger than Frederick; some fine houses, not many. We saw Mason's house, now used by the field officers of the Fifth Connecticut; the shops and stores are almost empty, but will probably revive rapidly. We took dinner at Taylor's Hotel, a pretty large house; a great many officers there. While we were in town, a skirmish took place on the Strasburg road four or five miles from town, resulting in our capturing between twenty and thirty prisoners: we saw them marched into town, some in uniform, some not.

* * *

CAMP SOUTH OF STRASBURG, March 28, 1862.

You must be expecting, by this time, to hear some account of what we have been up to for these last ten days. I will give you a journal of things as they have happened.

Last Friday afternoon, our brigade received orders for a four days' march to Centreville, fifty-five miles across the Shenandoah and over the mountains; the Second brigade had gone the day before; the First was to follow us. Our brigade formed line and started at ten Saturday morning, and made a good march of fifteen miles to Snicker's Ferry on the Shenandoah, passing through Berryville; we camped there. Reveille the next morning was beaten at five o'clock; at seven, things were moving; our regiment that day being put in the rear of everything. The Third Wisconsin, Twenty-ninth Pennsylvania, and Twenty-seventh Indiana, had crossed the bridge and half the supply train was over, when a refractory team of mules succeeded in making a bad break, two mules were drowned, and of course our chance of crossing was small until the bridge was repaired.

It was near night before it was ready, and we were ordered to camp again where we were. Reveille Monday morning at five o'clock. Mounted orderlies coming at the gallop brought us news of a fight at Winchester. Our march was countermanded and we were ordered back with a section of artillery and some cavalry to Berryville. Here we stayed, guarding the approaches till noon, when the rest of the brigade came up. Starting at about one, we marched back to Winchester, arriving there just before dark. Our regiment was quartered in some empty warehouses. We officers had the ticket office of the railroad for our quarters. I will give you now an account of the skirmish and fight of Saturday and Sunday, as I have heard it from eye-witnesses and from soldiers engaged. A few hours after the First and Third brigades had marched away from Winchester, Colonel Ashby, with a few hundred cavalry and a battery of artillery, drove in the pickets of General Shields' division, and came with his force almost into town ; our side pitched in and took a good many prisoners ; no great harm was done except that General Shields had his arm fractured by a shell grazing it.

That night, every precaution was taken to guard against surprise. The next morning, the enemy again appeared in small numbers, and there was cannonading on both sides throughout the day till three o'clock, when their infantry appeared. Our line was formed and the fight began. We had six regiments engaged : their force must have been between seven and eight thousand. The fighting was of the fiercest description for two hours, when the rebels gave way and retreated, leaving in our hands two hundred and forty-two prisoners, and between two and three hundred dead on the field and several hundred wounded. Our loss was about a hundred killed and four or five hundred wounded. The rebels fought as well as they ever can fight. They were close to their homes, numbers of them living in Winchester, and we whipped them by sheer hard fighting at short range. Persons who were near by told me that for two hours there was not an interval of a second between the firing of the musketry Captain Carey, of our regiment, whose company is on provost marshal duty in Winchester, had a pretty hard duty that night; he had to provide quarters for the wounded of both sides as they were brought into town. All night long they were brought in by the wagon load, every empty house and room in town was filled with them; the poor fellows had to be laid right down on the floor, nothing, of course, being provided for them. Monday they were gradually made more comfortable, yet as late as Monday night, when we arrived in town, there were numbers of wounded who had not seen a surgeon.

Tuesday morning, I went into the Court House, which had been turned into a hospital. In the yard, there were two cannon which we had captured; one of them was taken from us at Bull Run and belongs to a battery in our division. Just in the entrance were about twenty of our men that had died, laid out in their uniform for burial, their faces covered by the cape of their overcoat. The sight inside was of the most painful description; there were sixty or seventy of the wounded in the room, mostly of the enemy, and the most of them very severely wounded. Generally they did not seem to suffer much, but there were some in dreadful agony. I saw one nice-looking young fellow that I pitied very much. He could not have been more than sixteen or seventeen years old, and was mortally wounded, shot through the body. He was sitting up resting against the wall; his eyes were closed and there was almost a smile on his face. You could see, though, by the deathly color of his face, that he had only a few minutes to live. It seemed hard that he should have to die there with no one near that knew him. There was one rebel captain who was shot across the forehead, blinded and mortally wounded, who, when our surgeon attempted to help him, slapped him in the face and said he wouldn't let any " damned Yankee " touch him; he relented, however, in the afternoon and had his wounds dressed. I will say this for our two surgeons, they worked nobly for nearly twenty-four hours without rest.

During the day, the ladies of the town brought a great many comforts to the wounded of their side, but everything was refused for particular individuals, and they became more charitable and gave a great deal of aid to the surgeons.

One of the rebel wounded was George Washington, of the present Sophomore class at Cambridge; as he was brought in, he recognized Lieutenant Crowninshield, who was his classmate, and spoke to him. G. W is of the old Washington family and, of course, one of the " F. F V's." He was serving as a private; he has been made a great hero of in Winchester; he is said to be mortally wounded.

About ten o'clock, after visiting the hospital, Captains Savage and Russell and myself walked out to the battle-field, four or five miles from town. On the road as we approached it, were the marks of shells, dead horses and cows lying about where they were struck. At the side of the road where our artillery turned off, we found one of our men, the top and back of whose head had been entirely knocked off by a shell. The hardest fighting was along a ridge which the enemy attempted to hold. Along it for nearly a mile, the bodies of our soldiers and those of the enemy were scattered thick, although most of them were the enemy. In one little piece of thick woods, there were at least thirty of the enemy lying just as they fell; they were sheltered by a ledge of rocks, and most of them were shot through the head and had fallen directly backwards, lying flat on their backs with their arms stretched out in an easy, natural manner over their heads. Some were terrible to look at, but others looked as peaceful as if they were asleep. Men killed by a shot scarce ever have an expression of pain on their faces. It is astonishing how much less repulsive the bodies were that were lying about in this manner, than those that were regularly laid out in rows for burial.

The countrymen about here had, when we visited the ground, taken every button and other article of value off the bodies. I saw one who had had a daguerreotype cut out from a case that was hanging around his neck; almost all had had their boots taken off their feet. A number of people were out from Winchester, trying to recognize their townsmen. The bushes and trees here were completely riddled with bullets; there was not a twig the size of your finger that was not cut off, and trees the size of a man's body had every one at least three or four bullets in it. Our men shot remarkably well, as these things go to show. Several soldiers of Captain Carey's company got passes and went out to the fight and joined the Seventh Ohio; they fought well and took two prisoners and two rifles.

One of Captain Quincy's company, who was taken prisoner at Maryland Heights last year, and was released about a month ago, arrived at Winchester, on his way to join the regiment, the day of the fight; he went out to the battle and took a prisoner and a gun. At six o'clock that night (Tuesday), we got marching orders; at seven, we were on the way to Strasburg; we marched thirteen miles to just the other side of Middleton, arriving there between one and two A. M. We built fires here and lay down till daylight, then proceeded on to Strasburg, where we marched into a wood to bivouac. There was a good deal of sleeping done that night although we lay on the ground with nothing over our heads. Thursday morning, as we were quietly sitting around our fires, we heard the long roll beaten at the guard tent. An attack had been made on our outposts, and all disposable forces were marched in that direction. After going four miles, the firing stopped. Our brigade was halted in a fine wood where we are now camping.

CAMP NEAR EDINBURGH, April 7, 1862.

As I write less often now, you must expect me to be more voluminous, and I shall stick to my form of journal, as it may be interesting to me as well as you, some of these days, to have a connected history of our small share in this campaign.

The Saturday following my last letter, our whole regiment was ordered to go on outpost duty. We started about four o'clock and relieved the Twenty-ninth Pennsylvania. By the way, at this time our regiment consisted of only eight companies, Company G being on provost marshal and off at Centreville, and Company A being at Snicker's Ferry guarding the bridge over the Shenandoah. I had command of Company D, Captain Savage was sick. Three companies were held in reserve, the other five, B, D, E, H, and K, formed the pickets, furnishing the outposts and sentinels. We did not get our men posted till dark, and then it began to storm, raining, hailing, thundering and lightening. My company did not have the slightest shelter, and at the outposts no fires were allowed. The rain froze as fast as it fell, giving everything a coating of ice; altogether it was what might be called a pretty tough night. Morning came at last, and then I found that we were within a hundred yards of a big barn full of hay and straw; of course I moved the company right into it and had big fires built in front of the door, making things seem quite comfortable. The next thing to do was to push out the outposts and sentinels; this I did in connection with the other officers, until we came in sight of the enemy's vedettes. They do all their outpost duty in our neighborhood with Ashby's cavalry. It is an interesting sight to see their line of horsemen slowly walking back and forth on a ridge, standing full out against the sky.

About nine o'clock, Company F was sent out to make a reconnoissance of their position, but was driven back by a large force of cavalry. In the afternoon, they ran a gun down to within a mile of us and fired a few shells; one of them burst within a few yards of one of my men, but did no

damage. We were relieved in the afternoon by the Third
Wisconsin.

Monday night, we were waked up to draw and cook
rations, and received orders to march in the morning. At
nine next morning, our line was formed; our brigade had
the advance of all. As soon as we came in sight of the
enemy's vedettes, the column was halted : five of our companies were deployed as skirmishers, H, C, F, B, and I, forming a line a mile or more wide. As we advanced within
rifle range, they fell back; wherever they had any woods to
take advantage of, they would stay on the edge and fire at
us as we came across the open, but they shot very badly,
most of their bullets going over our heads. One of Company I received a bullet in his breast-plate, bending it all
up and passing through his overcoat, dress coat and shirt,
inflicting a slight wound. Occasionally they would give our
men a chance to fire, but very seldom, though we managed to
kill several of their horses, and, I think, wound some of their
men. Going through Woodstock was very lively : the rebels
planted their battery in the middle of the street, and shelled
away at our main body until our skirmishers almost flanked
them. One of our shells went straight through a church
steeple and through one wall of the jail.

We marched thirteen miles, the shelling and firing con-
tinuing the whole way. The enemy burnt their bridges as
they retreated ; there were four splendid railroad bridges
burned in this way We almost caught them at Edinburgh ;
the two bridges across Stony Creek had not been on fire
fifteen minutes when we arrived. The enemy, knowing we
could not ford that stream, took up a position and shelled
away at us, but our battery silenced them in less than a quar-

ter of an hour, firing with great accuracy right into the middle of them. One of the Third Wisconsin was killed here, and three or four others slightly wounded. It seemed impossible that we should get off with so small a loss ; the shells seemed to strike everywhere except where our men were. My good boy Hogan knocked one of their cavalry out of his saddle at nearly five hundred yards; he is quite a hero now in the company. As night came on, the firing ceased and we went into bivouac near by. The day was a very exciting one, and though it really amounted to nothing as a fight, on account of none of our men being hurt, yet it was good practice for us and gave us confidence under fire. Our pickets along the river are in sight of the enemy's all the time.

Last Friday our company was detailed to accompany some signal officers up one of the mountains of the Blue Ridge, to establish a signal station. We had a hard climb of it; the mountain was very steep, the view on top superb. You could see up and down the Shenandoah valley for miles ; could see some of Jackson's camps and a section of a battery within a short distance of our outposts; most of his force is concealed by woods. That night we bivouacked about half-way down the mountain. Our position was so isolated that we did n't dare to have any fires, but we did not mind much, as the night was warm and the moon bright. I thought, as I lay down, how impossible it would have been for me to conceive of being in such a position a year ago. It was the wildest place we have ever been in, the nearest house being a mile or more off.

Towards morning I was awakened by hearing the pleasant sound of rain-drops pattering around my head; a delightful sound, you know, when you have a roof over you, but not so pleasant when there is nothing between you and the clouds. There was nothing to do but pull my blanket over my head and sleep until daylight. No signalling could be done that day, so we marched down the hill and put the company in the nearest barn : we officers took a room in an adjoining house. Sunday was a beautiful day, and we again ascended the mountains. Monday I returned to camp.

April 9th, 1862.

As the mail has not yet gone, I open my letter to write a few more lines. We had a sad accident happen to our company this morning. We were returning from picket from across the Shenandoah : the river was very high and running like a mill-race. The only means of crossing was in a small flat-boat which would carry but six ; the boat was making one of its last trips, when a man named Freeman, sitting in the stern, gave a jump, capsizing the boat ; four of the men swam ashore, but Freeman and our fourth sergeant were drowned ; their bodies have not yet been recovered. It is a very sad loss. Sergeant Evans was a faithful, intelligent man, and we shall miss him a great deal. The storm of sleet and rain still continues; everything and everybody looks miserable and uncomfortable.

CAMP " MISERY," TWO MILES SOUTH
OF NEWMARKET, April 21, 1862.

The name of our camp did not originate at headquarters, but it is the most appropriate one I can think of for it. The regiment has been here for three days without tents, on a bare field. with no other shelter than what the men could rig up out of rails and straw. The rain has been pouring down in torrents most of the time, making the whole surface of the ground a perfect mire. We are lying around, like pigs, in straw. with wet blankets, wet feet, wet everything, and a fair prospect of nothing for dinner. We have had some pretty tough times lately, but this knocks everything else higher than a kite' I think even Mark Tapley would get credit for being jolly here.

Last Tuesday our company went on picket. I was stationed just at night at a barn on the extreme outpost on the edge of Stony Creek. The following morning I went out, taking Hogan with me, to make a little reconnoissance of the enemy's pickets. It was foggy, and I couldn't see more than a hundred yards. All of a sudden the sun came out and the mist disappeared. I had hardly brought my field glass to my eyes. when pst — pst — pst — three bullets came past me. One cut a sprig off a pine tree over my head : another struck a rail of the fence I was sitting on : the other went into the ground. You may have seen the Ravels execute some pretty lively movements, but the one that Hogan and I made to get behind the fence beat them all.

As soon as we were under cover we looked for our enemies. None could be seen, but Hogan shifted his position, exposing himself a little and drawing their fire again. This time I saw the smoke come from behind a fence about two hundred and fifty yards off. I saw at once that we could not touch them. The nearest cover from where we were was about one hundred feet away : that place had got to be reached in order to get back to my post ; I waited some time before I could make up my mind to exposing my valuable life, but I got across safely in this way: I put my cap on the point of my sword and raised it over the fence; their bullets struck in the rails all around it. Hogan fired a shot where the smoke came from, and then we ran for it! I tell you, I never felt more comfortable than when I got two thicknesses of a barn between me and the other side of the river. In the barn there was a little window; one of the men was taking aim to fire, when a ball struck his hand, inflicting a slight wound and tearing up his sleeve for six inches. Four other bullets struck the barn, going in one side and out the other. After that, I kept the men entirely out of sight, and no more harm was done. To give you an idea of how well they can fire, one of our sergeants put a board in sight, which they took for a man's head, and they put three bullets through it.

We returned to camp towards night. Reveille sounded the next morning at two-thirty. At four A. M., we started, and marched all day over the most confounded roads, constantly fording the streams, the bridges being burnt. Our movement was off on the flank; Shields's division moved straight down the pike. At one time we were within two hours of Jackson's army, but they got away. After twenty-two miles of the hardest marching we've ever had, over mud roads, we got into bivouac about nine P M. I had nothing but my overcoat, but I never slept sounder than I did that night on the leaves. I don't know whether I ever told you that I had been appointed ordnance officer of this regiment; such is the fact. Early Friday morning I started out to look up my three ammunition wagons. I found my armorer, who told me they were stuck fast about seven miles back on the road. Colonel Andrews, on hearing this, ordered me to take a guard and go back to them. This was pleasant, but no help for it. It took us till Saturday night to get those wagons up to this present camp, which is between Newmarket and Sparta.

✌ ✌ ✌

CAMP NEAR HARRISONBURG,
April 28, 1862.

Yesterday having just completed the usual Sunday inspection, we received an order in hot haste to get ready at once with one day's rations to make a reconnoissance. Our regiment, the Twenty-seventh Indiana, and eight hundred of the Vermont cavalry, formed the party. We went out on the Gordonsville road about nine or ten miles and drove in the rebel pickets, forcing them to display near two thousand cavalry and four regiments of infantry; this showed pretty plainly their position, and our object was accomplished. Jackson has apparently been reinforced by about five thousand troops, and is now in an entrenched position just the other side of the south fork of the Shenandoah, with a bridge between us and them, which has been stuffed full of combustibles ready to burn on our approach. We took two of Ashby's cavalry prisoners, and one of our cavalry was killed.

After a hard twenty-mile walk, we got back to camp about eight P M. Our division (General Williams's) marched to this place last Thursday, eighteen miles from Newmarket. We are now distant from Staunton twenty-five miles, and from Gordonville sixty-five. The enemy have saved us the trouble of going to the former place by turning off on the Gordonville road. I suppose by this time some of General Fremont's force must be in Staunton.

STRASBURG, May 14, 1862.

I never expected to write another letter from this place during the war, but so it is. After ten days' marching and countermarching, crossing the mountains into the other valley and coming back again, we have got here again, after an absence of nearly two months, without having accomplished the first thing during the whole of that time. We line officers have drawn up a paper to be sent to the Secretary of War, begging to be transferred to another division; one copy to be forwarded to Charles Sumner, and another to Judge Thomas. A somewhat similar one is going to Governor Andrew asking his assistance. They are all ably written, and I hope they will help us out of this.

The other day, when we were over the other side of the mountains, one of Captain Abbott's men disappeared from his company. Last night he came into camp in secesh uniform. His story was that he was taken about fifty rods from our bivouac by two of Ashby's cavalry and two infantry; that they carried him about twenty miles to Jackson's main force, and then promised him they would send him to a place where he would never see Yankee-land again, but he balked them by escaping their guard one night and keeping in the woods until he got inside of Colonel Geary's lines.

I dare say you have noticed, in the paper, that our Adjutant's clerk was shot, the other day, as he was marching between Mount Jackson and Edinburgh. He was a long distance ahead of the regiment; there were three shots fired; one minie ball struck him, passing through his right arm into his body, grazing his lungs, coming out the other side; he is still living, but his recovery is doubtful. We have had three other men disappear lately, very likely shot in this same way. An orderly was fired on, the other day, but not hit : he chased the bushwhacker, wounded him and caught him.

I had one piece of good luck when we were over in the other valley. I was out with the company on picket : early in the morning, I discovered three contrabands with as many horses just outside our lines. I had them brought in before me : one of them had a beautiful brown mare which took my eye amazingly : I offered the darkey five dollars for her, and he took me up. I sent the other horses in to brigade head-quarters by the contrabands.

.⁂ .⁂ .⁂

WILLIAMSPORT, May 29, 1862.

I take the very first chance I have to let you know I am safe and well. I did not cross the Potomac until last night. I was left there with a small detachment of men to support a battery. My hands are full to-day of ordnance business, so I must stop. I will write in full in a day or two.

.⁂ .⁂ .⁂

CAMP NEAR WILLIAMSPORT,
May 29, 1862.

I am going to start to give you a detailed account of what has transpired during the last week : whether I shall be inter-rupted or not, I cannot tell. Last Friday, after dress parade, I went out for my usual ride with Jim Savage. We met an artillery man, who cautioned us about riding outside of the camps, as they had just had a man shot by guerillas within a

short distance of camp, and several others had been fired at.
This shortened our ride. No sooner were we back at camp
than we heard of an attack at Front Royal. The Third Wisconsin of our brigade was immediately ordered over there.
At half-past two that same night, we were roused and ordered
to strike tents and pack wagons at once. From that time till
daylight, we sat around waiting further orders ; none came
till Saturday at ten A. M., when the whole division started
down towards Winchester. After marching five or six miles,
one of Banks' aides came galloping back from the front to
order up a battery, saying that the enemy were right ahead of
us attacking the wagon train. We halted for a short time,
but the alarm proved to be false ; only one wagoner had been
shot by a guerilla, but this was sufficient for Banks to make
up his mind that the wagons were safer behind than in front.

We kept on in this way till the town of Newtown was
passed. Soon after, we halted, and a section of Cathran's and
a section of Best's batteries were sent to the rear. In less
than fifteen minutes a brisk cannonading commenced, and
our regiment and the Twenty-seventh Indiana were ordered
double quick towards the sound of it. We found the wagon
train in a perfect heap in and on each side of the road, some
wagons tipped over, and a great many deserted by their
drivers. The men were allowed here to take off their knapsacks and overcoats which were left piled up in the field under
a guard. The rebel cavalry ran as soon as we deployed, leaving a good many killed and wounded by our shells. The
enemy were drawn up (how many we do not know) just beyond Newtown, with cavalry stretching out on each flank ;
they commenced the skirmish by shelling us ; the second shell
wounded two men of Company A. We took up a good posi-

tion on each side of them, with the artillery on each flank.
We fought here with our artillery for nearly two hours until
our wagon train was fairly started and most of it in Winchester.   Then, just as it began to get dark, the artillery and the
Twenty-seventh Indiana filed away and left us alone to cover
the retreat to Winchester.   Companies A, B, C and D were
thrown out as skirmishers : hardly were we out of town than
the enemy's cavalry and artillery dashed in, with a tremendous yell of triumph.   They attacked us at once.   We fell
back without any hurry, firing all the time, till we got to a
little bridge the other side of Cairnstown, where half the
regiment made a stand while the other half got their knapsacks.   The rebels here closed right around us : they were so
near we heard every order, and were able to make our dispositions accordingly.   There was not a word spoken in our
regiment, by officer or man, above a whisper, and it was so
dark that nothing could be seen except by the flashes of our
muskets.   Finally, we heard the order given to the rebel
cavalry to "Charge!"   A square was instantly formed in the
road, and the skirmishers rallied on each side.   The rebels
came thundering down the road, literally making the ground
shake.   Not a shot was fired until they were within fifty yards
of us, when Major Dwight gave the order. "Rear rank, aim!
fire! load!   Front rank, aim' fire! Charge bayonets!"   But
the bayonets were not needed.   Men and horses were rolled
over together, breaking the charge and sending them back in
confusion.

   This was the last attack of their cavalry that night: they
fell back and their infantry took their place.   The firing here
was very heavy, but we finally drove them back again after
losing about twenty of our men killed and wounded.   The

men had now all got their knapsacks, and we again started back. All of the wounded that could walk were sent on ahead towards Winchester, but nine had to be carried into a house to wait for ambulances. Colonel Andrews wouldn't abandon these, so we halted again, throwing out a strong guard in every direction. It was now eleven o'clock, the men were tired out, having been up for twenty-four hours. They sank right down in the road and a great many went to sleep, I among the rest. I don't know how long it was, but we were awakened by a tremendous volley being poured into us from almost every side, and for about a minute I could hardly collect myself, but I gave the orders for my platoon, which was then in the rear, to "dress, face about and fire!" I lost two men by their volley, both badly wounded. We were obliged to abandon our dead and wounded here and Doctor Leland was taken prisoner.

At one A. M., Sunday morning, we reached the bivouac of our brigade, stacked arms, lay down tired enough, to get a short sleep. Our total loss that night was somewhere about twenty or thirty. Company I suffered the most severely, losing about twelve.

I have been as minute as possible in describing this fight because I believe that we saved the entire train from destruction and kept the whole rebel force in check. Great credit is due to Colonel Gordon, Colonel Andrews and Major Dwight; the latter especially displayed the most perfect bravery and coolness. The men never obeyed better on drill or parade than they did under the hottest fire; they behaved splendidly throughout the whole.

At daylight on Sunday, our cavalry picket was driven in and soon afterwards the infantry: still no orders arrived as to the disposition of our brigade. Finally, after the rebel infantry began to deploy, Colonel Gordon would wait no longer and ordered us into line. On the right, the Second Massachusetts succeeded by the Wisconsin Third, Pennsylvania Twenty-ninth, Indiana Twenty-seventh, then came Colonel Donnelly's brigade consisting of the Fifth Connecticut, Forty-sixth Pennsylvania, and Twenty-eighth New York. In all, seven regiments not averaging six hundred men apiece. We had three first-rate batteries, and one or two regiments of cavalry that might just as well have been at home for all we saw of them. We had no sooner taken arms and faced to the right, than the infantry commenced firing. Not many of our men were hit, and we moved steadily on till we reached our appointed place. Meanwhile, the batteries on each side were keeping up an incessant roar. We attacked the two regiments opposite our position and drove them away. Two companies, G and D, were then deployed as skirmishers to attack the the battery in front of us; their fire was so well directed that the guns were abandoned by the gunners, but the rebel infantry pressed them (Companies D and G) so closely that they were withdrawn by Colonel Andrews' order just as the Twenty-ninth Pennsylvania and the Twenty-seventh Indiana came up to their support. These latter fired a few volleys; then, as two rebel regiments came out of the woods, prepared to charge them, but before they had fairly started, *seven* more regiments emerged from the woods stretching almost down to Winchester. The firing was then tremendous, and, I am sorry to say, the Twenty-seventh Indiana broke and ran, every man for himself. The Twenty-ninth Pennsylvania filed off in good order at the double quick. Colonel Andrews gave the order: "Attention! battalion! About face' By company right wheel!'" We marched away from the enemy in ordinary time, company front, in the most perfect order. The rebels instantly took our former position and commenced a pelting fire; they were within short range, yet almost all their shots went over our heads, otherwise our regiment would have been destroyed. It was cruel to see our poor fellows shot through the back and pitch forward on to their faces, as we marched down the hill. As soon as we reached the town, we took the first street on our right hand, and there formed line. Then it seemed to be first discovered how completely we were out-flanked and the strong probability that, in a few minutes, their artillery would be posted in our rear, cutting off all avenues of retreat.

We were then again faced to the left and started on the double quick through the town. Meanwhile, the enemy had gained the Martinsburgh pike parallel to the street we were on, and were pouring a heavy fire on us through the side streets, and numbers of men fell dead here that can only be accounted for as missing.

After getting out of town, they again began with their artillery, throwing grape and canister. Here the retreat was better organized: the whole division formed into five parallel columns, two or three hundred yards apart, all going on the double quick. We continued this for a considerable distance when, having passed all their flanking batteries, the lines were closed in more to the centre, the artillery and cavalry formed in the rear, and we went on in ordinary time. This was the last I saw of any fighting, although there was a constant firing in the rear of us. We marched twenty-three miles to Martinsburgh without a halt. There we rested for about ten minutes, then marched on to the Potomac, thirteen miles further. We brought up here between seven and eight o'clock P M., after twelve hours' incessant marching. From twelve o'clock Saturday noon till seven o'clock Sunday night, we had marched sixty miles,* been in two severe fights, had only three hours' rest, and had scarcely a particle of food.

Our loss in the regiment, as well as it can be ascertained to-day (Friday), is nineteen killed, forty-seven wounded, eighty-three missing. None are considered killed unless they were seen dead by some one. We were the last regiment that left the field from the right flank, and the very last in Winchester. I forgot to say that the United States store-houses were in flames as we passed by them, and the heat was perfectly terrible. The loss in our company was eleven.

Monday morning at three o'clock, I was roused by the Adjutant and ordered to report with Company B, together with Companies A, K, and E, and two companies of the Third Wisconsin, to Lieutenant Colonel Pinckney of the Third Wisconsin, to act as rear guard and support to a section of Cathran's battery and some cavalry, while the wagon train and troops crossed the river. We were in this responsible place till Wednesday night, when we were relieved. It was a most anxious time, as the enemy, in what force we did not know, were within a mile of us and we were receiving constant alarms from our cavalry. The first night, we kept our men under arms all the time, tired as they were. However, we got safely across Wednesday night, and I had the pleasure of taking my shoes and clothes off and getting a little quiet sleep for the first time since last Friday night.

* The actual distance from Strasburg to the Potomac is 54 miles, but including countermarching and movements on the field, the total distance marched was not much less than 60 miles.

Our greatest loss is the poor Major, but he may turn up yet. The men think everything of him and speak constantly of the "bully little Major." Captain Mudge is at Frederick, shot through the leg. Lieutenant Crowninshield is at Williamsport, shot in the leg.

⚘ ⚘ ⚘

CAMP NEAR WILLIAMSPORT,
June 3, 1862.

Last night, as we officers were sitting around our tents after supper, we suddenly heard a shout from the further side of the camp of "Major! the Major!" which was instantly taken up all over the field, followed by a rush of the men towards the guard tent; we all followed, and, passing across the lines, discovered the Major coming up the hill to camp, in a little old wagon. I wish you could have heard the shout the men set up when he fairly came in reach of them. They finally made a rush at him; it seemed as if they would tear him to pieces in their eagerness to touch his hand or some part of him; every cap was off and every face was on the broad grin. When he did get through the men, Colonel Gordon got hold of him and shook his hands and hugged him in the heartiest and most affectionate way; so he was passed along until all had given him a greeting.

After a short time spent in congratulations, Major Dwight returned to the men, who had not yet dispersed and were watching his every movement. He made a short speech, and then proceeded to give an account of *every* man of the regiment who was killed, wounded, or a prisoner. He had attended the burial, himself, of all of our dead, and had

visited the wounded, who were all doing well. He was able
to contradict entirely all stories of the rebel soldiers' cruel-
ties; they had not killed a single wounded man, but had
treated them kindly; the citizens were much worse than the
soldiers. When he spoke of Company I and their large number of killed and wounded, he said he could not help asking
for three cheers for their gallant conduct at the Kernstown
bridge on Saturday night: they were given with a will.
The Major mentioned each of the wounded by name, and had
something pleasant to say about almost every one relating to
some little peculiarities. which the men understood.

After Major Dwight had finished, Colonel Gordon made a
few remarks, ending by calling for three cheers for the Major.
Three times three and a "tiger" were given, and the men
dispersed, happy as they could be. One of the pleasantest
things that has developed by our late action is the kindly
feeling shown by the men to the officers; they have learned
their dependence on them. and have confidence now in their
pluck and willingness to share every danger with them.

We received a great deal of interesting information from
the Major, — none more so than this: Major Wheat, of a
Louisiana battalion, told Major Dwight that on Saturday
night their loss must have been ten to our one, and he wanted
to know what regiment it was that was ambuscaded all along
the road; he said that after their cavalry had been driven
back, the Second and Fifth Virginia regiments had been
ordered to the front, and it was with them that we did most
of our fighting that night. Their loss was very heavy, including a number of officers.

Major Dwight was taken prisoner in Winchester; he had
just helped a wounded man into a house and was surrounded

by rebel cavalry before he could get away. He surrendered in the cool manner he does everything. He made friends with everybody and succeeded in getting paroled; he left this morning for Washington with his brother, to try and effect his exchange. Drs. Stone and Leland have both been unconditionally released. L. is still at Winchester, taking care of our wounded. The correct statement about our company is, one killed, four wounded, and twelve prisoners. Jackson and his army are disheartened; they did not entertain a doubt but that they would capture Banks and his division, bag and baggage, and then make a foray into Maryland, but by good luck, we got out of this scrape with pretty whole skins. Captain Mudge is at Frederick; his wound is very painful. Crowinshield will be able to be moved in a few days and will go home. Major Dwight saw over a hundred of *their* dead buried Sunday.

I have just come in from a brigade review, almost melted: two mortal hours have we stood under a scorching sun, ready to drop.

✵ ✵ ✵

CAMP NEAR WILLIAMSPORT, MD.,
June 5, 1862.

You see by my heading that we are still on the wrong side of the river, but we shall be so for only a few days longer. I will mention some of the narrow escapes that came under my notice. Bob Shaw was struck by a minie ball, which passed through his coat and vest and dented into his watch, a very valuable gold one, shattering the works all to pieces, doing him no damage with the exception of a slight bruise: the watch saved his life; he has sent it home. A private in our company was struck in the forehead by a ball which cut a groove right across it, doing no harm and making an honorable scar. Another of our men was struck down in the street at Winchester by one of Stuart's cavalry; the sabre glanced on his cap and inflicted only a slight wound in his head; he was passed over as dead by the cavalry; he then quietly got up and escaped through a side street and across to Harper's Ferry. A corporal in my platoon, Saturday night, was raising the rammer of his piece to "ram cartridge," when a ball came between the fingers holding the rammer cutting into each. You remember Sergeant Lundy of whom I sent home a daguerreotype; well, he was cut off from the regiment by some cavalry, but managed to hide from them and get on to the Harper's Ferry road. Soon after, he caught sight of three of Ashby's men sitting by the side of the road; he got close to them, then presented his piece and told them they were his prisoners, and they were brought by Sergeant Lundy to our camp, where they were delivered over to the Provost Marshal.

One of our privates named Fagan was shot through the arm, and walked all the way to the Potomac that day; he is one of the best men in our company, only about eighteen years old. Another, named Stevens, was struck in the back by a piece of a shell, knocking him down, but only slightly wounding him; he got up with a smile on his face and was making some joke about it when another ball passed through First Sergeant Hatch's coat and into his hips, wounding him severely; he fell and I thought at the time he was killed, but I know now he is safe in the Winchester hospital. There were dozens more similar cases, but I have told enough to show that bullets were pretty plenty that Saturday and Sunday. The thing that strikes everybody most forcibly after a battle is, how it can be possible for such a small proportion of the bullets to produce any effect.

I suppose you have heard of Charley Horton's having his horse shot under him. He was close by our company at the time, the horse, a large gray one, was struck by two balls, one passing through his head, the other through his body.

I am happy to say that Gordon is going to get a brigade at last; he deserves it more than any Colonel I know of. This makes Captain Savage, Major; George Bangs, Captain, and me, Senior Lieutenant; and probably First Sergeant Powers, of Company H, Second Lieutenant. I hope that Gordon will get this brigade and Green will be transferred.

* * *

CAMP NEAR NEWTOWN,
June 14, 1862.

After about eighteen days' absence, here we are back again in Virginia, camped on the identical piece of ground where the fight raged the fiercest on Saturday night, the 24th of May. We crossed the Potomac the 10th, Tuesday, and bivouacked on this side of the river; the next morning we started early, six o'clock, and marched to Bunker Hill, twenty-two miles, camping there that night: the next day we marched twenty miles to this place. Our march through Winchester was with closed ranks, band playing "John Brown," "Yankee Doodle" and "Dixie," and our old Harper's Ferry flag flying, almost torn to pieces by the bullets of the Twenty-fourth and Twenty-fifth. People scowled as we marched through town.

As I said before, our camp is on the ground occupied by us in the first skirmish of Saturday night, and what is a still more striking coincidence, our mess tent is pitched on the exact piece of ground that our skirmishers rallied on when they poured in such a deadly fire to the rebel cavalry. The last man of ours that was killed here was buried close by, by a citizen. Yesterday afternoon, I rode back to Winchester and over the battle field. The effects of the artillery were still very apparent: stone walls and fences knocked to pieces, trees cut off, etc. Near where our right was, are three graves of our men who were killed there.

I had a very pleasant visit to the hospital where our wounded are : they are mostly looking very well. It does one good to see how they brighten up when one of their officers comes into the room where they are. I believe I spoke in one of my last letters about a private named Stevens, in our company, whom I saw wounded, first by a piece of shell, then by a bullet. The poor fellow is dead : I could not find out any particulars about him yesterday, only that he died in hospital June 4th. He was a very good boy, not more than eighteen years old ; he was one of the recruits that joined us last fall ; he always did his duty faithfully, and was a brave little fellow. It seems sadder about him because he had an older brother in the company, who always took care of him when anything was the matter. He has been very anxious since the fight, and now the first news he has received is of his death. It is a severe shock, but he bears it bravely, and says he feels happy that his brother never showed himself a coward.

CAMP NEAR FRONT ROYAL,
June 19, 1862.

Yesterday we struck camp about eleven o'clock, and at noon started off ; we marched about thirteen miles and camped this side of the Shenandoah. To-day we are on picket on the Middleton road, in quite a pleasant place.

* * *

CAMP AT NINEVEH, NEAR FRONT ROYAL,
June 24, 1862.

I don't think I have ever mentioned in any of my letters anything about the Third Wisconsin regiment. We have camped alongside of it now since the last of March. It is, without exception, the best regiment we have ever seen, leaving out our own ; the men are in good discipline, and the officers are gentlemen. For about a month, most of us of the Second have boarded at their mess-table ; it is a very pleasant one. Colonel Ruger sits at the head. He is one of the finest gentlemen I know, a graduate of West Point. If we had a few more such regiments as this, our army would be very different from what it is now.

* * *

CAMP NEAR WARRENTON,
July 12, 1862.

Last Sunday our division broke camp, and after a tedious day's march, accomplished only about five miles, the whole day being used up getting the wagon train across the Shenandoah. The weather was fearfully hot, equal to the famous eighth, last July. When we formed line before going into camp, many men fell fainting in the ranks.

Monday, we made an early start, and crossed the Blue Ridge through Chester Gap. The scenery was beautiful, but the weather was fearful; we camped for the night in a fine wood near the village of Flint Hill. Next morning we went on, five miles farther. to near Amesville. We stayed there until yesterday, when we marched to this camp, two miles west of Warrenton. All along our route, the men have almost subsisted on cherries and blackberries, both growing in the greatest profusion here; the men would fill their quart dippers in less than ten minutes.

We have got into a new country in appearance; the mountains have entirely disappeared and given place to splendid, great rolling hills and valleys, with beautiful woods scattered over them. The views that you get in this State are certainly wonderful in their extent. From the top of a comparatively slight elevation you can see for a distance of twenty miles all about you. I think that there is to be a large army concentrated here, and that, then, we are to move "On to Richmond," by the present indications; there is already considerable force here and it is increasing.

I rode into Warrenton yesterday with Bob Shaw and Dr. Stone; we found the place a great improvement on most southern towns. There are some very pretty houses and well kept lawns and gardens in the vicinity. We took tea at the "Warren Green Hotel," regaling ourselves on iced milk and corn-bread, finishing the evening by smoking our cigars on the piazza. Just as we were coming away, Charley Horton arrived with his General; it was a great mutual surprise to us and a very pleasant one. We have received orders to-day to turn in all tents except a limited number for the officers, to send away all trunks, each officer to keep only a small valise and roll of blankets. Regiments, etc., are also to keep constantly on hand ten days rations, so you see we are all ready for a long march ; don't care how soon it comes if it carries us towards Richmond! I am acting Adjutant for the present, but shall not be appointed, as Colonel Andrews says the time will be too short before I get my promotion, to make it worth while.

* * *

CAMP NEAR WASHINGTON, VA.,
July 18, 1862.

We are experiencing a long, severe rain storm, which is attended with the usual discomforts in camp. With the men, it is particularly hard, as they have now lost their comfortable Sibley tents and have only small shelter tents in their places, which afford them very little protection. Wednesday, just at dinner, we received orders to march at once. We were off in an hour's time on the back track towards Gaines Cross Roads. We went only a distance of five or six miles, crossing Hedgeman's River ; the rain poured most of the time in torrents : it cleared off at sunset and we had a beautiful rainbow. We were on the road the next morning by five o'clock. The day was terribly hot and sultry, but at noon the rain began again and fell by pitchers-full for several hours. We marched fourteen or fifteen miles to Washington, a small village on the Luray road. The fields by the roadside were as usual filled with blackberries, and, as we had frequent rests, every man had a share of the fruit.

The cause of our retrograde movement was this: General Pope's adjutant general sent an order to General Banks to take up a strong position with his corps near Warrenton; instead of writing Warrenton, he should have written Washington, so we had thirty-five miles' extra marching for nothing: one man's mistake causing several thousand to swear and wear out shoe-leather. We are encamped in line of battle, the batteries all in position; our line extends along a high ridge for a little over a mile. We are near the centre, supporting Cathran's battery. Our camp is on the side of the hill and commands a beautiful and very extensive view; the mountains are on every side, some close by, others blue and misty in the distance. Right below us on the level is the little village, quite a pretty one, almost hidden by trees. The whole country half way up to the top of the mountain, is covered by either wheat or fine woods, so that there are no bare, unpleasant looking spots. Before camping, there was directly behind our line a field of fifteen or twenty acres full of wheat stacks: an hour afterwards the field was there, but every stack was gone and every man in the division had a comfortable bed. Mr. Secesh was saved the trouble of threshing his grain at the expense of a good many barrels of flour.

I suppose that you have heard that Captain Underwood has been commissioned Major in the Thirty-third Massachusetts. If this is so, there is speedy promotion ahead for a certain first lieutenant. Don't address me yet as Captain of Company I; it might be embarrassing before I get my commission.

❦ ❦ ❦

CAMP NEAR LITTLE WASHINGTON, VA.,
August 2, 1862.

While you were quietly enjoying this Sunday morning among the mountains, our corps d'armée was out in a large field being reviewed by our new commander, General John Pope. The review passed off as most reviews generally do, terribly tiresome and tedious to the officers and men engaged, but rather a fine sight to outsiders. I was not much impressed by the appearance of our new general, but shall keep my mouth closed about him until he does something.

We have lately become acquainted with a new horror of war. The other night, we were all awakened, about one o'clock, by the most awful screams and groans, proceeding from directly behind our tent. We all rushed out and found Tom, Captain Williams' servant, apparently trying to tie himself up in a knot, all the time holding on to his ear for dear life, exclaiming, between his groans, "Oh! take him out! take him out of my ear! I shall go crazy!" and such like ejaculations. We found out at last that some kind of a beast had crawled into his ear while he was asleep, and was now working around near his tympanum, making him suffer the most horrible pain, if we could judge by the noise he made. The doctor came at last and took him to the hospital, and by pouring oil into his ear, killed the bug; he then gave Tom some morphine to make him sleep. In the morning, after a vigorous syringing into the afflicted ear, the animal hove in sight and was removed by a pair of pincers. It proved to be a hard, round pointed black beetle about *three-quarters of an inch long*. We all now stop our ears with cotton wool every night, not caring about having explorations made so near our brains.

We had, this last week, besides other drills, two corps d'armée drills and one brigade drill. Banks manœuvered the corps and did pretty well, except that he gave some rather original orders. It was rather a fine sight to see the whole corps formed in squares with the artillery in position, and to add to the interest, a squadron of cavalry charged some of the squares to try their steadiness; they thundered down on our regiment at full speed, not stopping until they fairly touched the points of the bayonets, but they didn't stir one of our men. The sight is really quite frightful, and it is easy to see that if the charge is not broken by a good fire, that the infantry would have to go under, but we know by experience, that the effect produced among the horses by the shots is very great. General Gordon is fast making his brigade a fine one; it is now altogether the best in the corps.

✿ ✿ ✿

On Picket near Culpepper,
August 13, 1862.

At last I believe I have a chance to write you an account of our doings during the last few days, and to relieve all your anxiety about myself. Last week Wednesday, our army corps marched from Washington, making about fourteen miles under a terribly hot sun; the next day, we went on five miles further to Hazel River. Friday night we made a moonlight march to Culpepper. Saturday morning, we started away again at ten o'clock towards the Rapidan River, leaving everything behind us, knapsacks and all, taking only two days' rations and plenty of ammunition.

We were ordered to the front to support General Crawford's brigade; following our brigade was General Augur's division, consisting of two small brigades, the whole making up Banks' army corps; we formed line of battle about six miles from Culpepper in a very strong position, our brigade on the right and Augur's division on the left. Nothing occurred until about half-past three in the afternoon, when a cannonading gradually began, increasing every minute until our entire left became engaged. From our position, we could see all that was taking place, and it was a sight that I shall never forget, to see two lines of infantry gradually approach each other across an almost level plain, both under a heavy artillery fire. As they drew near enough, we could see them exchange volley after volley of musketry; then everything became enveloped in smoke and we could see only whether our line advanced or retreated by watching the colors. It was easy to see that the men were falling fast by the constant lines of ambulances that we saw going and returning from the field.

About five o'clock, Crawford's brigade moved up in front of us and became engaged. The firing of musketry now became tremendous. We could see nothing of it in front on account of an intervening hill. At about six o'clock, our brigade (Second Massachusetts, Third Wisconsin, and Twenty-seventh Indiana), was ordered up on the double quick to relieve Crawford, his brigade having been literally cut to pieces by the terrible fire of the rebels. After going about a mile over the hardest kind of swampy and wooded ground, we reached the edge of the woods and came under fire. We marched steadily along, our whole flank being exposed, and took a position behind a low rail fence, the men being ordered to lie down. I will give you an idea of how things stood at the time. General Augur's division had been obliged to fall back to their original position and was now disengaged. Of General Crawford's brigade which went into the fight two thousand strong, twelve hundred had been killed, wounded or taken prisoners; the small remainder was rallying at some distance from the field, so there was nothing left to fight the rebels with but our three small regiments. Crawford met with his great loss in charging across the open field lying between the woods. General Gordon was ordered by Banks to do the same thing with our brigade; Gordon protested against it as an impossibility without supports, and finally gained his point.

At first, we sustained a fire from the rebels only in the woods, which was not very severe, but soon the enemy made their appearance in an oblique line and commenced a cross fire which was perfectly fearful. The Twenty-seventh Indiana gave way almost at once; the Third Wisconsin stood it nobly and did not fall back until the enemy was almost in their rear. In our regiment, not a shot was fired until Colonel Andrews gave the order "Commence firing!" which was not until the rebels were within two or three hundred yards of us. The effect was tremendous; we actually tore great gaps through their ranks, and their whole right was wavering; if we could have had any support at that time, we might have charged and driven their line like sheep, but that wasn't in Banks' programme. Meanwhile, the roar of musketry was perfectly deafening; the noise of the bullets through the air was like a gale of wind; our poor men were dropping on every side, yet not one of them flinched but kept steadily at his work.

Sergeant Willis of my company (I forgot to say I was in command of Company I), who was acting first sergeant, stood directly in front of me; he received a ball in his head and fell back into my arms saying, " Lieutenant, I'm killed! " and almost instantly died; he was a very handsome young fellow, and as he expired his face had a beautifully calm expression. I laid him down gently on the ground beside me and had hardly done so, when one of my corporals named Pierson, who was touching me on the left, was shot almost in the same place, but not killed. It is impossible to relate all the incidents that took place; it seemed as if only a miracle could save any one. I received two bullets through my trousers, but wasn't scratched. Colonel Andrews was splendid! He kept riding from one end of the line to the other, giving his orders coolly, as if on drill; his horse was wounded twice.

I never was more surprised in my life than when I heard the order to retreat. I did not know what had taken place on our right, and could not understand what it was for. With Lieutenant Abbott's assistance, I managed to help Lieutenant Oakey off the field to the hospital; he was quite severely wounded. Our regiment formed behind the hospital, about a quarter of a mile from the field, the rest of the brigade joining us. It was not until I saw the regiment in line that I began to appreciate our loss. Major Savage had been left severely wounded on the field; Captain Abbott, dead: Captains Carey, Goodwin, Williams and Quincy, Lieutenants Perkins and Miller, wounded and left behind; Lieutenants Robeson, Grafton, Oakey, Browning and Surgeon Leland,

wounded and brought off, and Captain Russell missing, and
our regimental line was not more than half its usual length.
The only officers left were Andrews, Adjutant Shelton, Captain Bangs, Lieutenants Pattison, Choate, Fox, Abbott and
myself. Our colors, those which the Boston ladies gave us,
had five bullet holes through them: the eagle was shot off
and the staff was shot through by a minie ball, splintering
it into two pieces: our color-bearer, Sergeant George, brought
off the whole of it. This is the second flag we have had honorably used up in battle.

Soon after forming our second line, I was detailed by the
Colonel to go to the hospital to take charge of sending off
the wounded. A house with quite a large yard had been
taken for hospital use: the scene in and about it was very
painful. Soldiers lying in all directions, with every variety
of wounds. I took hold and worked hard, loading the ambulances, for about an hour, when our regiment moved and I
was ordered to join it.

Our brigade now took up a position on the left of the
line of battle, to do picket duty, Ricketts' division being
on the right. Our sentinels were close to the rebels and
we had continual skirmishes throughout the night. We
had one man killed, and took several of the rebel cavalry
prisoners. Once the enemy crept down on us, as they did
that night at Newtown, and poured a volley over us, which,
luckily, was too high and did no harm. Morning came at
last, after, to tell the truth, a pretty nervous, disagreeable
night. Daylight showed us that large reinforcements had
arrived and that we were now in a condition to fight, but the
day wore on, still no attack was made by the enemy. Banks'
division was in reserve.

The battle I do not consider a victory to either side; we held our original position and they theirs, the ground between being neutral. Our brigade was withdrawn from the field about noon and bivouacked in a wood near by. I was sent into Culpepper on official business for Colonel Andrews. The town seemed to be one great hospital, every hotel and private house, almost, being used for that purpose. I saw Robeson, Grafton, Oakey and Browning; they were all suffering considerably from want of attention: the first is wounded in the wrist, the second in the forehead, the third in the hip, and last in the thigh, a very severe, dangerous wound. I got back to camp early in the evening. Soon after, Lieutenant Abbott, Mr. Quint and a burial party, left for the battle field to perform the last duties for our poor men. Abbott returned early in the morning and brought the shocking and sad intelligence that Captains Abbott, Carey, Goodwin and Williams and Lieutenant Perkins, were lying dead on the field, and that a number of our wounded were still there. I was sent right off with all our ambulances to the field. The scene there was too awful to attempt to describe; very few of the dead had been buried, and they were lying thick in every direction. Captain Carey had lived nearly twenty-four hours and looked as natural as if alive.

I had the bodies of all the officers put into the ambulances and sent them back to the regiment: the wounded also were all cared for. I then went over to the rebel lines with Bob Shaw, under a flag of truce, to see what could be heard of Harry Russell, the Major, Captain Quincy and Lieutenant Miller. We met some very pleasant rebel officers who were very gentlemanly and kind, and found out from them and some other sources, that Russell was unhurt and a prisoner, Quincy and Miller wounded and prisoners; we managed to get some money to Savage and Russell.

Our loss, as it stood yesterday morning, was as follows :—

5 Commissioned officers killed, 8 wounded, 1 prisoner.

25 Enlisted men killed, 97 " 33 missing.

30 killed, 105 " 34 " Total 169.*

We carried into action twenty-two commissioned officers and four hundred and seventy-four enlisted men, a little more than one out of three meeting with some casualty. In Company I, there are, one sergeant killed, one sergeant wounded, one corporal wounded, nine privates wounded and one missing. Yesterday afternoon, Banks' army corps moved back to Culpepper to reorganize. I was sent out on picket immediately after arriving last night, and am taking the opportunity to write this long letter. I have not had my clothes off since last Thursday night, so you can imagine I am not very pretty to look at. I am a full-fledged Captain now, and have got my commission. I shall be assigned to Company B, if possible.

Poor Captain Williams! I saw him standing perfectly erect only a few minutes before he was shot, and ran over and spoke to him. His was the next company to mine. He will be a great loss to us all.

*　*　*

NEAR CULPEPPER, VA., August 19, 1862.

Yesterday afternoon came orders to our corps, directing wagons to be instantly packed and sent to the rear, and

---

* The actual loss was 58 killed and mortally wounded, 101 wounded, 15 prisoners not wounded. Total loss 174.

our men to be provided with three days' rations, and to be
ready to march at a minute's notice. We were bereft of our
tent and all other luxuries, but no movement commenced
until about half-past eleven P M., when we started and
marched about a mile, then halted and are still halting, for
what purpose Pope only knows. Last night, for the weather
was fearfully cold, we kept as close around the fires as we
would in winter. I have just had some bread and butter and
peaches for breakfast, and am now enjoying a good cigar, so
I shall be fortified against whatever may turn up to-day
From what I can learn, this is the nature of our movement:
Pope has found that his army is not quite large enough to
take Richmond, and is going to let the enemy once see his
"back," and find out that a "line of retreat" may be very
useful by falling back as far as **Warrenton** and concentrating with McClellan.

Orders to "fall in" and "march."

*   *

RESTING NEAR BULL RUN,

August 29, 1862.

I resume my narrative again like a shipwrecked mariner,
hoping at some distant day I may be able to send it to you.
Since the twenty-first, we have been marching and countermarching, manoeuvering and skirmishing, almost constantly,
in all that time not having quarter rations or more than one
or two whole nights' sleep. We have really suffered hardships, now, for the first time; we have known what it is to
be grateful for a drink of the muddiest of water and for a
half of a hard cracker and an ear of corn or a green apple for

dinner, and to be able to lie down and get two hours' quiet sleep. Last night, I took off my shoes, washed myself and got a *whole night's* sleep for the first time in ten days; this morning, I had a beefsteak, a cup of coffee and a piece of hard bread for breakfast; I feel now like starting again, and shall probably be gratified before long.

For six or seven days, we skirmished along the Rappahannock, moving constantly from one point to another of the river, generally marching in the early part of the night, stacking arms at eleven or twelve o'clock, and lying down on the ground until daylight to catch a little sleep, half the time not being able to take our blankets from our horses for fear of a sudden move. At daylight, cannonading generally began, either by our batteries or others along the river. One morning, we had a pretty lively time; our battery (Cathran's First New York), became engaged with two rebel batteries and, for an hour, we saw and heard the smartest artillery fighting we have heard yet. At the end of that time, the two rebel batteries were silenced and withdrawn; four of our Parrotts were burned out and rendered unserviceable, and a number of horses and mules, and one man, killed. The solid shot and shell came tearing through the woods where we were supporting the guns, in great style, making the branches fly; one tree was cut down close to where Colonel Andrews was. Fortunately, none of us were hit, though the noise of the shot and shell was terrific.

Day before yesterday, our army was withdrawn from the river on account of a movement of the enemy to our rear. We reached this place last night, after two days' toiling along after Sigel's wagon train, over the dustiest of roads, under the hottest of hot suns. Two days ago, a battle was fought near here, in which we were victorious; the graves of some thirty of each side are in the field; this is all we know of the fight.

Last night a fight* began which is still going on, four or five miles north of us, where the enemy seems to be in force. Everything seems to be upside down and wrong end to. I have not heard a man yet wild enough to suggest how it is all going to end. The enemy are certainly using the most desperate measures to capture Washington and invade Maryland; they may be successful, but I trust not. The whole of McClellan's and Pope's army is near by somewhere, and there are large reinforcements around Washington. We don't feel very anxious now, except about our next meal. Somehow or other, officers and men seem to keep up their spirits wonderfully through all these hard times, and I hope will continue to, as there is nothing I can see now to change the times. Hogan and the mare are safe and perfectly invaluable in this emergency. Rumors come to us now that Jackson is at Centreville with his whole army.

*　*　*

BIVOUAC BETWEEN
CENTREVILLE AND BULL RUN,
September 1, 1862.

We have been moving around for the last two days in about the same style as heretofore. Yesterday morning, we were routed out early and marched, by a very wide detour, thirteen miles to this place, the enemy having pushed a large force between us and our main body. We were fortunate to

---

* Second battle of Bull Run.

get off as safely as we did, as the enemy came into our old camp as the rear of our column moved out of it. We had to destroy a railroad train nearly a mile long, to prevent its falling into their hands. There was any quantity of clothing, hospital stores and nice things furnished by the Sanitary Commission, on board; all these were burned. I can't learn anything about what has taken place the last few days; I only know we have been fighting severely. I judge, by our movements, that our left has been driven back. We have passed over two battle-fields in our marches; one of them covered some of the old Bull Run ground. We passed yesterday some of the winter quarters of the rebels. Their houses looked very comfortable, but of all dreary places on the face of the globe, I cannot imagine a drearier one than the Plain of Manassas. For miles and miles, almost to the Rappahannock, these great rolling plains extend, some times covered with woods, but mostly with high, coarse weeds and rank grass. There is very little population, only a house here and there at intervals of a mile or more.

*   *   *

NEAR DARNESTOWN. September 10, 1862.

I have time to write a word to say that I'm safe and well. We are on the move all the time and have not had a real rest yet.

I have been considerably used up with fatigue, but am feeling better now. We are with Sumner's corps and have been beside the Twentieth Massachusetts several days. I expect we shall see some some fighting in a day or two. We move toward Frederick in about half an hour.

MARYLAND HEIGHTS, September 21, 1862.

To go back a little; last Sunday, we marched through Frederick. almost the last corps of McClellan's army. We marched to the sound of the cannon to Middletown Heights. reaching the latter place about half-past one Monday morning, after the battle had been fought and won by our men. We lay down on the ground and slept till daylight.

Monday we marched to within about five miles of Sharpsburgh. Tuesday we united our corps to the main army. A battle was expected that day, but nothing took place beyond a little shelling. We were aroused that night at ten o'clock and marched to our position on line, reaching it between one and two A. M. We were just behind Hooker's division. There was continual picket firing throughout the night.

I awoke at daylight with the full conviction that we were going to fight a battle that day. The first thing to do, of course, was to eat a good breakfast. which I fortunately had with me. I had scarcely finished before the cannonading began, followed quickly by heavy musketry volleys. We got under arms at once and our corps marched forward. We halted just before reaching the field, while our gallant general, Mansfield, gave the orders for our disposition. He was a splendid old veteran; fine white hair and beard. He had commanded us for three days only, but we all felt his good influence. The poor man received his mortal wound before we had been under fire five minutes.

Our brigade moved up into an apple orchard; we had the right. The Third Wisconsin was engaged first, receiving a tremendous fire; we were quite well protected. Captain Mudge was slightly wounded, and about a half a dozen men.

Our regiment was now called upon to support the Third Wisconsin. We formed a line almost at right angles with theirs, and poured a heavy cross-fire on the rebels, who were in a cornfield not a hundred yards off; this continued about ten minutes, when the rebel line broke, turned and ran. Our brigade now advanced with a tremendous cheer; the whole field before us was literally covered with dead and dying; we took a number of prisoners from the rebels and the battle flag of the Eleventh Mississippi. We advanced in line for several hundred yards, then halted: our part of the work had been done for the present.

It was sad, now, to look around and see the shattered battalions that were left in the places of the comparatively full regiments we had seen an hour before. The Third Wisconsin had lost more than half its numbers, and almost all its officers; it was very much the same with the Forty-sixth Pennsylvania. Our loss had been very small, though I think our fire was altogether the most effective of any regiment. Colonel Dwight caught up our rebel flag and rode by our line, waving it triumphantly; every cap went off and a cheer went up that you must almost have heard at Jamaica Plain. It was one of our poor Lieutenant-Colonel's last gallant acts, and I don't believe many who saw him will ever forget it.

All of a sudden, Sumner's whole corps came up behind us; we gave them a cheer as they passed by. They were in three lines and looked splendidly. They advanced into a wood and were met by an awful fire; they returned it gallantly, but were unequal to their task and were obliged to give way to the right a little, leaving the woods to the enemy. All this time we were lying down flat under a heavy fire of solid shot and shell, which tore the ground up around us, but as usual did no harm.

Now came our turn again; Gordon's brigade was ordered to attack the woods on the right. We crossed a high rail fence into a lane* and ensconced ourselves behind the fence on the other side within fifty yards of the woods; we had on our right and left two new regiments. We had hardly taken our position when the rebel line came out of the woods, so near you could distinguish the features of the men. We gave them a volley which sent them back in quick time under cover of a natural breastwork they had there; then, without any cause, the new regiments bolted, officers [Sept. 22, 1862, The first sheet was written on picket: I was suddenly relieved and am now in camp in Pleasant Valley] and men, and we were left alone. We stood it for about ten minutes, losing a third of our men and several officers, when the order was reluctantly given to fall back. This we did in good order (though it was hard work getting over that high fence in our rear, with much appearance of dignity), for about a hundred yards, when the regiment was halted; then ranks closed up and again made ready for attack or defence.

Now, too, it was sad to look at our thinned ranks; I found I had lost two men killed and five wounded; many of the companies had suffered more severely, but our greatest loss was Colonel Dwight. I saw his horse shot, and saw him dismount and try and hold his horse by the head, but the animal struggled so violently that he broke away; almost immediately afterward, Colonel Dwight received his death wound. He was within six feet of Colonel Andrews at the

* The Hagerstown turnpike, which is quite narrow at this place.

time, and as he was struck and sank to the ground, said,
"That's done for me." As soon as our regiment halted, four
men immediately volunteered to bring him in; this they succeeded in doing, though all the time under a heavy fire. He
was carried to a farmer's house, but lived only about thirty-
six hours. Lieutenant Mills, acting Adjutant, was badly shot
through both legs; Crowninshield received a flesh wound
in the leg. Captain Francis was shot through the hand and
lost two fingers. Colonel Andrews' horse was shot through
the shoulder. Captain Shaw was struck by a spent ball in
the neck; Robeson was grazed in two places; I was struck
by a spent ball in the temple, which laid me on my back for
a moment and raised a pretty black and blue spot; I thought
at first it was all up with me, but I soon got the better of that
idea. We carried into action less than two hundred and
forty men and lost about eighty killed and wounded.* During the rest of the battle, we were on different parts of the
field supporting batteries. We lay down that night about
ten o'clock, glad enough to get a little rest. The dead and
dying were all around us and in our very midst.

At the first streak of daylight, I awoke; the first sight I
saw was a squad of wounded rebels coming into our lines:
you can't imagine such miserable looking objects as they
were; their wounds undressed, and bleeding, and their clothes
torn in tatters. I found that Bob Shaw and I had slept
within fifty feet of a pile of fourteen dead rebels, and in
every direction about us they were lying thick.

One of the most brilliant actions of the day was a charge
of Smith's division; they passed our left and swept the rebels

* Actual loss 18 killed and mortally wounded, 54 wounded. Total
loss, 72.

from their front like chaff. Our artillery was splendidly served and did great execution. Everywhere the rebels fought with desperation. Rebel prisoners stated that their army numbered over one hundred thousand, and that they expected to win the day and annihilate our army and have an open road to the North. Friday morning, we had been reinforced by at least thirty thousand men, and McClellan moved his whole army forward, but the rebels had gone, leaving dead and wounded on the field uncared for: the sight everywhere was dreadful, and one that I hope you may never see the like of; it cannot be imagined or described.

Our corps marched until two o'clock Saturday morning, over the roughest of roads and through the darkest of nights, reaching the summit of Maryland Heights ridge about ten miles from Sandy Hook; here we lay down till daylight, then marched along the ridge over rocks and stumps to Maryland Heights. Our old crowd had a nice dinner at Mrs. Buckles': it was very pleasant. I was sent out upon our old camping ground with my company to do picket duty. Here I stayed until Sunday evening, when I was relieved and marched my company down a breakneck road to the regiment which was bivouacking in Pleasant Valley. I arrived about nine P M., and lay down and slept under a blanket for the first time for a week. It was luxury enough, though there was nothing overhead but blue sky.

To-day we pitched camp and began our work with company books and papers, thinking at last we were going to rest; but to-night our hopes are dashed by an order saying, "Reveille at four o'clock; march at daylight." I am now sitting up to finish this letter, because if we move as we have been moving, it is actually impossible to write.

MARYLAND HEIGHTS, September 26, 1862.

In my last letter, I wrote that we had orders to march the next morning. Our whole corps was routed out before daylight; our division, under command of General Gordon, marched to Maryland Heights, our brigade occupying our old last year's camping ground. Green's division crossed the Potomac and now occupies London Heights, the other side of the Shenandoah. Sumner's corps is encamped on Bolivar Heights. I think at last we are going to have a little rest: I can't tell. Everything seems about as it did last year up here; we have as splendid views and fine sunsets as ever. We have been very busy making up our pay rolls for the last two days. They are now a month behind time; there is any quantity of other papers which have been accumulating for the last six weeks, which will keep us hard at work for a week at least.

One of the men of my company killed at Sharpsburgh, the other day, lived in Brookline, and had been out here only about six weeks; his name was Thomas Dillon, and he was a good, faithful fellow. He was buried by two men in my company who volunteered to do it. A letter came for him two days after his death, which I think, under the circumstances, was one of the most affecting things I ever read, and yet it is only one instance among thousands. I do not know of anything that has brought the horrors of the war more plainly before me than this letter. I have written to the father of Dillon, telling him of his son's death.

You remember, don't you, of my speaking of a young boy named Stephens, who was killed at Winchester; his brother was wounded at Cedar Mountain, and has since died; they were their poor father's and mother's only sons: it is one of the hardest cases I have known.

I have talked with a number of the rebel prisoners. You have no idea what innocent, inoffensive men most of them seem to be: a great many are mere boys; there are some old men, too, with humped backs. Scarcely any of them seem to have any idea of what they are fighting for, and they were almost all forced into the army. I talked with one poor little fellow from Georgia who had received a severe wound: he could not have been more than sixteen years old. He said that all he wanted was to get into one of the hospitals at the North; that he had been abused and knocked around ever since he had been in the army, and that the first kind treatment he had received and the first kind words he had heard were from our men. He expected to be bayoneted as soon as we came up. The more I see of battle fields convinces me that instances of cruelty to the wounded are extremely rare, and that they are treated, almost universally, with kindness by the men of both sides. When we crossed the field, we drove the rebels from where their wounded were lying everywhere; but our men took the greatest pains not to touch them or hurt them in any way, although sometimes it was almost impossible to avoid it. And when we halted, the men gave almost every drop from their canteens to the poor rebels. The idea that a soldier could ever bring himself to bayoneting a wounded man, strikes me now as almost absurd; it may have been done during this war, but I don't believe it.

Our wounded at Cedar Mountain were treated with the greatest kindness by the rebels; they gave them plenty of water and built shelters to protect them from the sun in many cases. This making out the Southerners to be a lot of cut throats is perfect nonsense ; their leaders give a great many harsh orders, but the soldiers are not responsible for them.

I wonder if R. knows that his class-mate and friend, Breck Parkman, was killed at the battle of Sharpsburgh, the other day. He was on some general's staff and was probably killed by the fire of our brigade. Charley Horton saw a rebel surgeon who told him of it.

I believe that we are in quite a permanent camp now. It must be so, I think, for the whole army has endured a hard campaign of six months and must have rest; neither men nor horses can hold out forever. Then we have our recruits to make soldiers of, and the new regiments need any amount of drill. But there is another thing also true, that we have only got two months more in which any work can be done before we go into winter quarters.

The best news that we have heard lately is that Harry Russell is at liberty and exchanged; we hope soon to have him back here with us. There is no one I feel more pity for than Major Savage; we heard that he had lost a leg and would probably lose one arm; I don't believe he can live through it. He is one of the finest men I ever knew; nothing coarse or rough about him. He had a very delicate constitution, but was so plucky that he would do his work when a great many in his situation would have been on the sick list. He was one of my intimate friends, and had been particularly so during the last few months before Cedar Mountain.

Captain Quincy is at last heard from, it seems, badly wounded and a prisoner at Staunton. I doubt whether he or Major Savage ever will rejoin the regiment again to do duty with it; if that is the case, Captain Cogswell will become

Lieutenant-Colonel, and Mudge will be Major. I shall be third Captain and shall have the colors. No one in our regiment can complain that he has not had promotion enough to satisfy him during the last few months. You will be pleased, I think, to know that a few of us have now got a first-rate " mess " in working order. It consists of Bob Shaw, Lieutenants Oakey. John Fox, Tom Fox, Abbott and myself. We have a really good cook, who can make good coffee, cook eggs in any way very nicely, and also make pies and puddings ; to roast and broil or stew is child's play to him, and although our cooking materials are of the most limited description, we have not, since we have been this side of the Potomac, had a poor meal.

We found it, in our last campaign, to be an unmistakable fact, that a horse couldn't stand as much marching as a man ; it got to be a common remark among the men on our march from Culpepper here, as we passed the dead or dying animals which had been abandoned, " There, we've killed one more horse : bring on some fresh ones, we're good for a few more yet."

ᴥ ᴥ ᴥ

MARYLAND HEIGHTS, September 29, 1862.

I rode over to Harper's Ferry, yesterday afternoon, with Bob Shaw and Charley Whittier (the latter you remember of the Twentieth ; he is now on General Sedgwick's staff). We went to Colonel Lee's headquarters and to the Twentieth regiment. I saw John Ropes's brother ; he is now Acting Assistant Adjutant-General to Colonel Lee who is commanding Dana's brigade.

There is a rumor that Andrews is going to be made Brigadier-General; it would be hard for us, but he deserves it.

MARYLAND HEIGHTS. September 30, 1862.

We have received, to-day, pretty conclusive evidence of the death of Major Savage: we have also heard that Quincy's chance for life is very slim. Hasn't the mortality among our old officers been dreadful? I cannot bear to think of it. If we lose Colonel Andrews, there will be very little left of the old Second.

To-morrow I go up on the mountain in charge of a large fatigue party to fell timber. I imagine there is going to be another fort built there.

MARYLAND HEIGHTS. October 6, 1862.

Everything continues quiet with us. We have a nice camp and are beginning to make ourselves comfortable. I have a floor in my tent and a patent bedstead of Hogan's invention. Our mess gets on finely; we have plenty to eat and very good too. I know you will be pleased to feel that I am no longer in danger of starvation. You'd hardly believe we had suffered any hardships lately, to see us after dinner or supper, sitting or lying around my tent, enjoying our pipes and cigars, reading the papers or having a quiet discussion on some subject.

Last week, we had a visit from President Lincoln, accompanied by Generals Sumner and Howard and a large staff of other officers. He reviewed our regiment briefly, we receiving him with the customary honors. General Sumner paid our regiment the handsomest compliment that I have heard come from any officer of high rank. He said, in our hearing, to the President. " This is the Second Massachusetts Regiment, the first regiment that volunteered for the war. I have it on good authority, General Sedgwick, that it is the *best* regiment in the service."

Such praise as this, coming from the source it does, is very pleasing. After the review, I was detailed (I suppose from my knowledge of the mountain paths and the fact that I had a horse), to guide the party to the summit of the Maryland Heights. I showed the way until we got to a path where it was right straight up, when Abraham backed out. I think it must have reminded him of a little story about a very steep place; at any rate, around they turned and went down the mountain. I gave "Uncle Abe" a few parting words of advice with regard to the general management of things, bade them farewell, and went back to camp.

I am afraid we have lost Colonel Andrews : he was detailed day before yesterday, to take command of a brigade of four new regiments; this is probably but an intermediate step before being commissioned Brigadier. Captain Cogswell is now in command ; if neither Major Savage nor Captain Quincy ever come back, he will be Colonel, making Mudge Lieutenant-Colonel, and Russell, Major, and me second Captain, Curtis' old place on the left of the line.

Has the death of Major Sedgwick been spoken of in any of the Boston papers? You remember he was formerly a first Lieutenant in our regiment : he left us last autumn to go to his cousin's, General Sedgwick's, staff, where he was made Assistant Adjutant General and promoted to be Major. We have seen a good deal of him since we left Washington. He was one of the most interesting men in conversation I ever knew, full of stories and experiences of the Peninsular campaign, in which he took an active part, having been present at most of the principal battles. The night before Antietam, he was around at our bivouac. We were discussing the probabilities as to when Richmond would be taken; I made him a bet of a basket of champagne that it wouldn't be taken the 1st of January, 1863. This wager he accepted and registered in my pocket book and signed his name to it. The next day was the battle. General Sedgwick went into it with his division in Sumner's corps; Major Sedgwick received his wound in that terrible wood where our right wing suffered its heaviest loss. The bullet went through his body, grazing his backbone, instantly paralyzing the whole lower parts. He remained on the field two or three hours perfectly conscious, though suffering the worst pain. During this time he wrote several pages in his book, requests, etc. He was removed to Frederick, Maryland, where he died two or three days ago. He was only one among many, but he was one of the original "Second," and a man I always liked very much.

I believe I have not told you about our old flag. Sergeant Lundy is color-bearer now (the old Crimean soldier of whom I sent the daguerreotype); he's a splendid fellow and plucky as can be; all through the action, he kept the flag up at full height, waving it to and fro. Well, on examination of it after the fight was over, we found *twenty new* bullet holes through the colors and three through the staff. The socket in which the butt rested was shot away close to the Sergeant's belt. Our old staff was shot in two at Cedar Mountain, and is now at home being mended. While I think of it, I must tell you of one most singular incident that happened the day of the battle. As we were advancing over one part of the field, which was pretty thickly covered by our dead and wounded, a man of Company F, Captain Mudge's company, suddenly came upon the dead body of his father, who was in the Twelfth Massachusetts Regiment and had been killed early in the day. It was a terrible meeting for father and son; they had not seen each other for over a year. The next day the son got permission to bury his father in a decent manner and put a head-board at his grave.

Have you made up your mind about the Emancipation Proclamation? At first, I was disposed to think that no change would be produced by it, but now, I believe its effect will be good. It is going to set us straight with foreign nations. It gives us a decided policy, and though the President carefully calls it nothing but a war measure, yet it is the beginning of a great reform and the first blow struck at the real, original cause of the war. No foreign nation can now support the South without openly countenancing slavery. The *London Times*, no doubt, will try to make out slavery a Divine Institution, but its influence does not extend everywhere. I think the course of that paper, since this war began, has been more outrageous than anything I ever knew of; you wouldn't think any paper could be so base as to say, as it has just said, that the President's Proclamation was published to produce a servile insurrection. It may have the effect to cause disturbances among the troops from the extreme Southern States, who will think, perhaps, that their presence is needed more at home than up in Virginia. There is no mistake about it, if the fact becomes generally known among the slaves of the South that they are free as soon as within our lines, there will be a much more general movement among them than there has been before. It is evident that Jeff Davis is frightened by it, to judge by the fearful threats of retaliation he is making.

Yesterday, Bob Shaw and I took a fine horseback ride of about twenty miles, visiting the vicinity of Antietam. Most of McClellan's army is encamped near there. We expected to find the First Massachusetts Cavalry, but they had moved up the river to Williamsport. My horse is in fine condition, now; she seemed to enjoy the exercise yesterday as much as I did.

♣ ♣ ♣

MARYLAND HEIGHTS, October 20, 1862.

To-night I am all alone and naturally feel a little blue, so my letter may not be very cheerful. Bob Shaw is on picket; so is Captain Robeson; Tom Fox is sick with a light fever down in Sandy Hook, and his brother has gone down to see him; my tent, therefore, is deserted. To-day I have been out again with one hundred axe-men; it is an interesting sight to see so many men at work at once felling trees; we began our labor at the bottom of a ravine and worked up a steep hill. Sometimes there would be as many as twenty or thirty fine trees falling at once; they reminded me of men falling in battle, that same dead, helpless fall. The effect was still stronger from the fact that the choppers were almost always concealed by underbrush. I very nearly lost one of my men in an accident to-day. He had just given the *coup de grâce* to a large, heavy ash tree, and had cleared himself from the fall of it, when another tree falling from above, struck it, changing the direction of the fall of the first and bringing it down with tremendous force where the man was standing. He attempted to dodge, but had not time and was thrown to the ground. I was near by, and ran up to him. I found him perfectly senseless, and I thought, at the time, dying. He proved to be a man of my company named Conlan, one of my very best soldiers, the only one that I mentioned as having distinguished himself by bravery at the battle of Antietam. I had him moved to a comfortable place and sent for our surgeon and a stretcher. After lying insensible for about half an hour, he came to himself for a little and was moved to our hospital. I was much relieved by Dr. Stone's telling me that there were no bones broken; his shoulders and back were terribly bruised, though, and it will be a long time before he gets about again.

Major Higginson of the First Massachusetts Cavalry made us a passing call the other day, on his way to Washington, arriving last Friday night about ten o'clock and taking breakfast with us and spending the forenoon Saturday; he gave us all the latest news of our friends in his regiment. They are having considerable work to do now, scouting about over the country. I had one of the pleasantest times, Sunday, that I've had for some time; after inspection, Shaw and I mounted our steeds and rode off into Pleasant Valley. The road was very pleasant and the day beautiful, a genuine October one, with a hot sun but a bracing air. The country is looking its best now, though the trees don't change here as they do around home. Yet there was some bright color on the sides of the mountains. We made our first call on Captain Charles Lowell at General McClellan's headquarters. We found Major Higginson there, and a Mr. Bancroft of Boston, who is visiting his friends in the army. After spending an hour very pleasantly there, we proceeded to accept an invitation we had received a few days before, to take dinner with a friend of ours, Johnny Hayden, of Captain Edwards' battery, Third United States Artillery. We met some pleasant, jolly officers there, who had been all through the Peninsular campaign. Of course, there were plenty of yarns told on both sides, and experiences compared. We had a nice dinner and rode back to camp at sunset satisfied that we had had a thoroughly good time.

Days like these are like oases in our ordinary dull routine, and they come rarely enough to be enjoyed.

So many of our officers are sick, absent or on some extra duty, that there are only about seven of us in the line left to do all picket and fatigue duty, bringing each one of us on once in three or four days. There are at least two hundred men detailed from our regiment every day now for guards, or other purposes.

❧ ❧ ❧

CAMP NEAR SHARPSBURGH, MD.,
November 2, 1862.

You see at once that our position is changed, although we are still on the Maryland side of the river. The orders we received at the time of my last letter were countermanded the next day, and another corps was sent across the river. Everything remained as usual for several days; Wednesday, I was sent on picket with my company up the canal to guard a length of three miles of the river. It was a beautiful October day, and I enjoyed the scenery along the Potomac very much; the trees on both sides were very brilliant. If it had

not been for the existing animosity between us and our
Southern brethren, I could have had some capital shooting,
as the river was full of ducks.

About eight o'clock, P M., the field officer of the day
paid me a visit and informed me that I was instantly to draw
in my men; that our brigade had received marching orders
and probably had already started. This was interesting, but
no time was to be lost. It was after nine when I left my
post, and after ten when I reached the old camp ground.
The regiment was gone, but one of the surgeons who was
left with the hospital told me that the brigade had moved
towards Sharpsburgh about two hours before. I was relieved
at once by this information, for I knew I could find them
there. After a little deliberation, I made up my mind that
it was best to spend the night where I was. The men found
no difficulty in making themselves tolerably comfortable in
the skeletons of their old houses with the aid of good fires.
I borrowed a blanket of the sutler and lay down on some
straw on one of our old tent floors. Towards three o'clock
in the morning, I woke up with awfully cold feet and amused
myself till daylight making a roaring great fire, burning up
our old bedsteads and other furniture.

Soon after daylight, I started with my command; after
between two and three hours' pretty smart marching over a
splendid road through a fine country, I came up with the
brigade bivouacking by the side of the road. Very soon, we
marched again to our present camp, where we relieved some
regular regiments of Sykes' brigade which were on picket
here. Our camp is in a beautiful open wood about five hundred yards from the river; we are on a sort of a perpetual
outpost duty. Our regiment guards the principal ford (run-

ning for three-quarters of a mile along the river). This takes a hundred per day for the actual guard; the remainder of the regiment acts as a reserve. The rebel cavalry pickets are on the other side within talking distance. They seem to be peaccably inclined, and I trust the murderous practice of picket firing will not be begun on either side. It would make the duty dangerous and uncomfortable; now we can ride along the tow path within pistol shot of the enemy without feeling any anxiety.

McClellan is probably pushing southward with his army. We have heard pretty heavy and rapid cannonading to-day in the distance. I wish now that we were with the army; if the main body of it is going through a winter campaign, I want to be with it. We shall not stay here if our forces occupy Winchester and the intermediate points, I feel sure.

Yesterday I had a mighty pleasant call from Major Curtis and a friend of his from Boston, Mr. Edward Flint; they took dinner with us and we had a very pleasant time talking over old experiences. I rode back with them to the place where Major Curtis is on picket with a part of his regiment, six miles above us. I took tea there and rode home by moonlight. I lost my way about three miles from here, among an endless number of wagon tracks, paths, etc., so I threw my rein on my horse's neck and she brought me across the fields in almost a bee line to our camp.

I don't know whether I mentioned, in any of my last letters, that we had heard, the day we were at McClellan's headquarters, that Major Curtis had been mentioned as having distinguished himself on the reconnoissance towards Martinsburgh, where he had command of the cavalry.

CAMP NEAR SHARPSBURGH, MD.,
November 11, 1862.

We had an interesting little reunion and supper at my tent last evening. Yesterday morning, Bob Shaw and I rode into Hagerstown where the First Massachusetts Cavalry are stationed, about fourteen miles from here. We found our friends there getting ready for a move, having a preliminary inspection of men, horses, etc., they having received orders to join Pleasanton. By dint of a little persuasion, we got Curtis and Higginson to ride back with us. We had already arranged a supper to which the five captains in the regiment had been invited; Cogswell, Bangs, Robeson, Shaw, and myself. We sat down immediately after "tattoo" and had a jolly time; there were seven of us, all original "Seconds." Of course, there were innumerable recollections recalled, many of them sad, but a great many very pleasant; old times were talked over and the many changes that had befallen us since our first Camp Andrew experience. The supper was very good; a capital soup, followed by roast quail and "fixings," claret, coffee, cigars, etc., all done up in pretty good shape for camp. An occasion like this makes up for many vexations, and we all appreciate it.

Last night we received the news that Andrews had been appointed Brigadier-General and assigned to Banks; so we have lost our second Colonel, as honest and faithful a man as ever lived. He is one of the officers in the army who has worked his way up himself, and has been promoted purely on account of his own merit without political influence or wire-pulling. By this promotion and the death of Lieutenant-Colonel Savage, Quincy becomes Colonel, Cogswell, Lieutenant-Colonel, and Mudge, Major. I shall be third Captain and have the colors, Savage's original place. Sawyer will be tenth Captain; at Camp Andrew he was tenth Second Lieutenant, twenty grades he has gone through.

That was a very good article you sent me, taken from the "Advertiser," about Colonel Savage. It was evidently written by some one who knew him well. It was perfectly true and did not exaggerate his good qualities an atom. He was nearer to being a perfect man than any one I ever knew

* * *

CAMP NEAR SHARPSBURGH, November 14, 1862.

I wonder if you are having as charming a day at home as we are having here. It is genuine Indian summer, with that soft, hazy atmosphere so peculiar to the season. The sun is almost hot, and only the chill in the air occasionally tells one how near winter it is. The leaves have nearly all fallen from the trees around us, and the river is almost in view from my tent door. Our camp must now be in plain sight from the other side, but I trust the rebs won't be so ill-mannered as to throw any shells into it.

Everything about our camp has the appearance of winter quarters; the men have, most of them, built themselves very comfortable houses of logs, boards, etc., with fire-places of various kinds in them, all far more comfortable than anything we had last winter. We officers are all fixed up in some shape or other, very pleasantly. I am living alone now and have my tent nicely floored; at the end of it, I have had the seam ripped up and have had built a good, open brick fire-place, so that now these cold evenings, and, in fact, nearly all the time, I have a fine blazing wood fire. You have no idea how cheerful this is; it seems almost like sitting down at home.

We heard, yesterday, the joyful news that Harry Russell had been exchanged. He won't allow much time to elapse before he joins the regiment. I know we shall all be glad enough to see him. He is one of our very best officers and a first-rate fellow; I hope he will never have to go through another such experience as he has had this summer.

You don't know what an interesting thing it is to ride over the hard fought ground of Antietam. Yesterday, Bob Shaw and I visited all the places where we were engaged, saw where our men were killed, etc.

We could follow our first line along by the graves; next to ours came the Third Wisconsin's, which lost terribly in this place; next to that was a battery which was splendidly fought. Where it stood, in one place there are the remains of fifteen dead horses lying so close that they touch each other. Farther on, towards our left, we found numerous graves of the Twenty-eighth Pennsylvania men; they were in a wood. Every tree in the vicinity is scarred by bullets, and the branches torn by shell and shot. No language could describe more forcibly the severity of the fight. It is hard to realize, in riding through these now peaceful and beautiful woods, that they could have been filled so lately with all the sights and sounds of a great battle.

CAMP NEAR SHARPSBURGH,
November 22, 1862.

Yesterday, I received the great box of clothing which has been the matter of so much interest with us all for the last few weeks. It was in perfect condition and everything was most satisfactory.

All my men are now well provided against the cold, and are as comfortable as they can ever expect to be while they are soldiers.

I forget as to who you told me was the knitter of that pair of patriotic stockings for Sergeant Lundy; she would have felt flattered if she could have seen the expression of thanks on his handsome face as I gave them to him. Hogan also received his pair, pleased at the distinction.

I cannot say for certain that some of the men with slim shanks and long feet didn't, in some cases, receive the stockings designed for thick ankles and chubby feet; but generally, the written instructions were followed out to the letter.

I have tried to write a note of thanks, but it is a very poor expression of them. You know that speech-making and that sort of thing were never in my line, but such as the note is, I enclose it with this epistle and you can circulate it among those of my friends who may be most interested in it.* I believe that the greatest share of the thanks belongs to you, and you must so take it.

---

* The note was as follows: —

CAMP NEAR SHARPSBURGH,
November 22, 1862.

I have received to-day the long-looked-for box of clothing which you have so kindly made and sent to my company.

I have felt very thankful to you all since I first heard of the interest which has been shown to serve myself and my men, but I never appreciated the extent of the gratitude that I owed you till I saw the amount of labor and pains that must have been bestowed to produce such a quantity of most excellent and comfortable clothing. I had my company formed

CAMP NEAR SHARPSBURGH,
November 30, 1862.

I have nothing very new or interesting to write to-day, except about an expedition we made into Virginia last week, which you may like to hear about.

Last Monday night, about nine o'clock, Captain Cogswell took seventy-five men of the regiment and marched quietly up the river about two miles. Captain Robeson and Lieutenant Grafton went with him; hardly any one else knew anything about the expedition. Captain C. had a guide who was thoroughly familiar with the country on the other side of the river. They crossed in three boats, having to make several trips, and proceeded at once to Shepherdstown and posted guards at the principal entrances to the town. Then with the main body, they surrounded two houses pointed out to

---

and marched to my tent, where I read your note, and then I commenced the distribution of the shirts and stockings; I first gave each man in the company one of each of these articles, and then to every sergeant and returned prisoner, or any one else who had seen especially hard service, another one, making as fair a division as I could. The written instructions found with some of the stockings were very entertaining and proved very useful in the distribution.

I believe that my men felt truly grateful to you for your kind present, and though a soldier shows very little emotion, whatever may occur, yet when they thanked me, I knew that they meant what they said. It must be some comfort to every man to know that while he is suffering hardships and dangers, he has kind friends at home who are thinking of him and administering to his comfort and happiness. You may be sure that it is a strong motive for us to do our duty bravely, knowing all this, and feeling that we have your best wishes.

Once more I thank you, each and all, most heartily, and hope that at no very distant day, I may do so in person.

them by the guide as the headquarters of the rebel scouts. At the door of one of these houses were five cavalry horses ready saddled and bridled; these were immediately taken; a party under Lieutenant Grafton then burst in the door and rushed into the lower rooms; four men were immediately secured; the fifth seized his arms and rushed out a side door. Captain Cogswell, on the outside, saw him and called out for him to surrender; this order was repeated several times, but no attention was paid to it. Captain C. then called to the men to fire on him; two shots were fired; the second hit him and he fell; almost before any one reached him, he was dead. He proved to be Captain Burke, a captain of scouts. He belonged to Stuart's command, and was on that General's staff; he was quite a famous character in this neighborhood, almost as much thought of by the people here as Ashby was by the inhabitants of Warrenton and the Shenandoah Valley.

After taking one more prisoner and a few arms, the party returned safely to this side of the river, arriving in camp between three and four o'clock, A. M. Tuesday noon, an order came for a similar party to go again to Shepherdstown for the purpose of paroling some rebel officers and men supposed to be secreted in the houses there, and to make a further search for papers and arms. This time, I had the good fortune to be detailed for the service, and had command of the infantry, the whole party consisting of seventy-five infantry and about twenty cavalry, Captain Cogswell commanding the whole expedition. We forded the Potomac just below our camp. The water was terribly cold, and between two and three feet deep; the bottom was rough and the stream fast. The river here is about three hundred yards wide; you may be sure there was very little fun fording it. We kept quietly along the Virginia side of the river for a mile, then made a quick turn up the bank and came suddenly on Shepherdstown; the cavalry dashed into the town first and gave chase to a few scouts that were there, but the latter escaped.

When we came up, the people, men, women and children, were all on the streets; they seemed to be in a state of great alarm. We made a rapid search through the principal houses and public buildings, finding quite a number of papers and taking and paroling three commissioned officers and twenty privates. Among the arms that were taken was one very good English double-barrelled gun, which I have kept and shall try to have some sport with, as quail are very numerous in this vicinity and I have made friends with the owner of a very nice setter.

We recrossed the river safely and the men were allowed a good strong whiskey ration to make up for their wetting. They enjoy these expeditions as much as anybody.

The people over there are in a great rage at the death of Burke and swear to be revenged on our regiment. The man who killed him belongs to my company; he is a new recruit, but a very smart one.

Thanksgiving passed off with us very pleasantly. My wine came all right and was very nice. We had a union dinner of all the officers of the regiment. The dinner was very good indeed, plenty of nice poultry, plum pudding, champagne, etc. We couldn't help remembering last year's dinner and the great change in officers since then, but there was very little sadness manifested and we had a very pleasant time. Charley Horton came up from Harper's Ferry and all General Gordon's staff were also with us. My company had a fine dinner I bought for them out of company fund; ten turkeys, six geese and twenty-four chickens and a barrel of cider; they had, besides, as much plum pudding as they could eat.

The chances for furlough have sunk to the lowest point; I don't think now there is hardly a chance for one. Captain Bangs is going to try the experiment of sending an application on to Burnside, but I don't believe it will be noticed. I am, of course, allowed the first chance, but I prefer to wait for about two weeks. General Gordon, you know, has been sent home quite sick; this hurts my chance considerably.

* * *

CAMP NEAR SHARPSBURGH,
December 9, 1862.

Orders have come to us this afternoon to prepare for a march to-morrow morning, with five days' rations, etc.

From what we can learn, we are going to cross the river at Berlin, and proceed via Leesburg to Fredericksburg, to join Burnside. Everything in camp, of course, is in apparent confusion, packing up, sending off sick, etc. It seems hard to leave this camp, where all is so pleasant and comfortable; the men are all nicely housed; we have first rate kitchens, everything seemed arranged for the winter, but it is no use regretting these things: we can stand a roughing as well as most of them, I think.

* * *

BIVOUAC NEAR FAIRFAX STATION,
December 15, 1862.

I will take the opportunity of a few hours' respite from marching, to let you know of my present whereabouts and good condition. We have arrived at this place after about five days' marching, making seventy miles from Sharpsburgh. We have been called up at half-past three every morning, and have not stopped until after dark any night, though our marching has been very much interrupted by bad roads, delays about the wagon trains, etc.

I met with the greatest misfortune, on my third day's march, that I have had during the war. Hogan started out about a mile ahead of the column, as was his usual custom, to forage for us; he had just got through a small town called Hillsborough, when a party of guerillas made a dash out from the side of the road, and before he had time to put spurs to my horse, they had ridden him down and seized him. They had hardly done this when our advance came in sight, and our cavalry saw them and gave chase. I saw the scamps as they rode off for their lives, but I had no idea, until nearly two hours afterwards, that my poor mare was among them. It was an awful blow when I did hear it; they told me that Hogan was between two of them; one held a pistol to his ear while they whipped the horse. The pursuit was vain, and I lost everything, Hogan, horse, saddle, bridle, overcoat, dressing-case, tobacco, rations and all. You can hardly imagine how badly I felt: to lose all my comforts and conveniences, and my poor horse also, was a great deal; but to have Hogan taken by a parcel of ruffians who haven't anything good about them, was worst of all.

Harry Russell and Bob Shaw have been very kind to me since this happened, lending me their servants and doing everything they could. Of course, our "mess" is now broken up, but we three stick together and sleep under the same blankets. We've had very good weather for marching and sleeping out since we started, being quite warm. We heard, yesterday, that Burnside had met with some success, but had been pretty badly cut up, and that fresh troops were being pressed forward in large numbers to the front. Our regiment is rear guard to-day ; it will be very late before we start, and after midnight when we get into bivouac.

* * *

BIVOUAC NEAR FAIRFAX STATION,
December 20, 1862.

I wrote, the other day, from near this place. That day we marched as rear guard over seven miles of the muddiest kind of Virginia roads, crossing the Occoquan creek ; we went into bivouac in a thick wood a little while after dark. We made our usual nightly arrangements, eating our supper of coffee, bread, etc., and spreading our blankets, and very soon lay down for the night. Towards morning, all three of us awoke simultaneously, with some large rain-drops spattering in our faces. We drew the rubber blankets out from under us and put them on top, and turned in again. I was next awakened by a perfect deluge of water pouring in on me from the blanket where it had collected ; as it was nearly daylight, I concluded to get up. About nine o'clock the rain stopped, and shortly afterwards we marched. The roads were in the worst possible condition, wagons sinking to the hubs of the wheels ; we went only three miles, then stopped for the day. The next morning (Wednesday) we started at daylight, and marched back to this place. If we hadn't got used to such things, the march back over these horrible roads would have been very discouraging. We learned, when we got near the station, that our division had been ordered back because that place had been threatened by the enemy. The most that could have been lost by losing that place would have been some fifty thousand rations, yet this seems to have been a sufficient reason for preventing us from joining the main army. We also learned here that Burnside had been entirely repulsed, and was again on this side of the Rappahannock. The rebels have paid us off now for Antietam. No one seems to have any idea what will happen next. I am more afraid of a disgraceful peace than anything else, from the looks of everything now.

⚜ ⚜ ⚜

CAMP NEAR FAIRFAX STATION,
December 22, 1862.

As my first announcement, I will tell you that Hogan is all right with the exception of being paroled. He arrived at camp last Friday, having been kept by the guerrillas three days. The terms of his parole are so strict that I asked him very few questions. He told me that one of the scamps appropriated my overcoat, and that another rode off on my mare the morning after her capture. He managed to save some of my letters which were in my coat pocket. I felt that it was dangerous for him to stay with us; so Saturday morning I sent him off to a parole camp, with all the good advice I could think of and five dollars in money. He will write to me of his whereabouts, and I shall endeavor to get him a furlough. We are still lying here, in a miserable state of uncertainty about our future movements; no officers' tents, nothing, in fact, to make us comfortable.

It has been very cold for the last two or three days and nights. You would be amused to see us, sitting around a fire trying to eat our breakfast or dinner before it freezes hard; dippers of water soon become iced, and yesterday we enjoyed the luxury of frozen buttered toast and frozen sardines. In washing, our hair becomes a solid mass before it can be brushed or combed. We have one comfort, that is, that we sleep warm at night.

* * *

FAIRFAX STATION, January 2, 1863.

Last Saturday night we suddenly received orders to march at a moment's notice, but we remained undisturbed that night. Sunday morning, about eight o'clock, we started off; our whole corps was posted in the Dumfries road, our brigade guarding the Wolfrun Shoals on the Occoquan. This was all done on account of a large rebel cavalry force coming up on our left flank; we were sent out to endeavor to intercept them, but they didn't come our way; they went around north of Fairfax Court House, having a slight skirmish there. Infantry will never catch cavalry in this country, and I hope they will give up attempting it before long.

We bivouacked that night near the Occoquan, and marched back to camp next afternoon. There was some very pretty manoeuvring, on the telegraph wires, between the two parties on Sunday. The rebels cut the wires at Burke's Station, and telegraphed to the commander of the post at Fairfax Station to "burn all stores, wagons, etc., and abandon the post." The officer in command suspected something wrong, and telegraphed back, "I have plenty of force to hold the place, more infantry and a battery of artillery will be here in an hour." The truth was, there was only one small regiment of infantry, the Third Wisconsin, and two pieces of artillery, and no chance of any more for a considerable time. This undoubtedly saved the station. A message was intercepted from the Quartermaster-General at Washington about a lot of mules. Stuart telegraphed back: "That last lot you sent me were not good; be more careful in future," and signed his own name to it. This raid accomplished nothing in our vicinity, and could be repeated any number of times; they know every road in the country, and every house contains a friend and spy to them. We could do the same thing in Massachusetts, though I hope we shall never have the opportunity. There is considerable fear felt in some quarters that this cavalry is to be followed up by a large force. Isn't it shameful that, at this late day, anybody should be trembling for the safety of Washington? But so it is! I don't know but what it would be better for the whole country if Washington was taken and burned. What we need is to feel that we are fighting for our lives and liberties; that is the way the rebels feel: they think that if they don't win, they will lose every liberty. Our people seem to be in an indifferent state, not caring much about it either way; they would like to see the South conquered, if it could be done by any moderate means; but when it comes to every man and woman making some great sacrifice, they don't think it worth while, and would rather have a disgraceful peace than a continuance of the war. They don't seem to see that in case of such a peace, to be a native of the North would be sufficient to disgrace a man, and that we should always be considered a whipped nation. Abroad, a Northern man would be despised, and rightly. I feel much stronger about the war than I ever have before, and certainly hope that I shall never live to acknowledge such a nation as the Southern Confederacy.

♣ ♣ ♣

FAIRFAX STATION, January 6, 1863.

We have at last moved into a new camp, and are situated very comfortably; the men have good log houses with their shelter tents pitched on top, four men to each house; the camp is laid out with great regularity and is a very creditable place altogether; the officers have A tents (seven feet by seven feet) pitched on log walls, averaging a tent to two officers. We have been at work about ten days on this camp and are as well off now as we were at Sharpsburgh; no one knows, of course, whether we shall enjoy these good quarters, but we hope to do so, through the coming wet weather. The weather for the last three weeks has been remarkable, not a single storm and no severely cold days.

We had a division review on Saturday, and another one on Sunday. The first day, I was Officer of the Day and did not attend, but I went Sunday; it was before General Slocum; Captain Russell was in command, Mudge being sick. The review was a very fine one, about the best I ever saw. General Slocum told our brigade commander that our regiment was by far the best in his corps and the best he had ever seen in the service. The men did look finely; their clothes, of course, are old and worn, but their rifles, belts, and brasses shone right out. What a pride one could feel in an army, if every regiment in the service could be depended upon as ours can for any kind of work. I haven't any doubt but with good officers we could have the best army in the world.

Rumor says that Burnside will ask to be relieved before many days. Who will be our next commander, no one knows; Lord save us from Hooker, at all events!

❧ ❧ ❧

CAMP NEAR FAIRFAX STATION,
January 10, 1863.

Our rainy season has begun at last, I think; to-day it has poured. Everything looks muddy and damp enough. If it continues for a week as it did last winter at this time, mark my words, there will be no more campaigning in Virginia this winter. We are well settled now in a comfortable camp, with a strong probability of staying here for a while.

I agree in part with what you say about the administration, but I don't fear an armed interference in six months or six years. I feel certain that England will do nothing but stand aloof and badger both the North and South, and it cannot be policy for France to quarrel with us, it seems to me. As for what foreign nations may think of the corruption of the Government, I don't care; I've made up my mind that there never was a government in time of war, European or any other on the face of the earth, that wasn't as corrupt as corruption itself; all history shows it. If Napier in his "Peninsular War" is good authority, there never were more dishonesty, knavery, and bribery in a government than there were in England's at that time. That war was managed, at first, till Wellington took hold of it, very much as ours has been; generals were interfered with as ours have been, and newpapers' stories and home criticisms were believed by the people sooner than official dispatches.

From the first of March to the first of June, I predict that there will be the liveliest fighting we have ever seen in this country, and with good fortune, we may end the whole war and have a happy and honorable peace. If we had any other than a conquered peace, I should never feel that I had done with my uniform, but should always expect war and fighting. If the South got its confederacy, I fully believe the States would be fighting among themselves in less than five years; it is the strong military government and their feeling about slavery that is binding them together so now; their strong feeling about States' rights is what they will break on. I think the weakest points in our own government are these very States' rights, which allow State Governors to interfere and dictate to the Central Government.*

❧ ❧ ❧

CAMP NEAR STAFFORD C. H.,
February 8, 1863.

What do you think of the First Massachusetts Black Infantry? I suppose there is no doubt but that the regiment will be raised; one of our captains † has had the offer of the colonelcy, and he has accepted it. As a military measure, I entirely believe in it, and I hope it will be entirely successful. It is ridiculous for persons to try and laugh this thing down;

---

* A ten-days' leave of absence was granted about this time and the writer went home accompanied by Captain Shaw.

† Captain Robert G. Shaw

there is no reason in the world why black troops raised in this country shouldn't be as good as those used by the English and French. I always argue that any men who have understanding enough to obey orders implicitly, where they are led by brave officers, can make good soldiers. I think negroes could be more easily disciplined than most white men. The understanding, of course, is that all the commissioned officers shall be white. If I had anything to do with such a regiment, I should not want to raise much of it in the North, but get enough men there to form a skeleton, and then go South and fill up with contrabands.

You will probably hear before long who the Captain is, that I have referred to; he doesn't want it mentioned at present.

No one pretends to have an idea about our next campaign here in Virginia. I hope and trust that we shall all find ourselves with our right on the James River by the middle of next month, and that the Ninth Corps led off in that direction to-day, but these are only my hopes; I have nothing to ground them on.

✄ ✄ ✄

CAMP NEAR STAFFORD C. H., VA.,
February 12, 1863.

Tuesday I rode over with Major Mudge to the First Massachusetts Cavalry; we found our friends there well and glad to see us. Lieut.-Col. Curtis has been laid up with a lame leg from a horse's kick, but was nearly right again. The same morning, Captain Shaw went off to go to work on his new command, the First Massachusetts Blacks. He has a hard piece of work before him, but I hope he will be entirely successful. The greatest doubts in my mind are whether the Northern negroes will enlist; I don't put much faith in them myself.

ᴥ ᴥ ᴥ

CAMP NEAR STAFFORD C. H., VA.,
February 14, 1863.

I have been appointed Provost Marshal of the corps, and shift my quarters to-morrow to General Slocum's headquarters. I am to have my company and another one from my regiment, and a company of cavalry for my guard. The duties I don't imagine to be very heavy, except in the office. I am allowed a horse and a wall-tent to myself. I rather like the idea of a change for a little while at any rate; if we begin active movements again, I shall try and get back to the regiment. I like General Slocum very well, from what I have seen of him, and he has some very good men on his staff. I shall probably see a good deal of them.

ᴥ ᴥ ᴥ

HEADQUARTERS TWELFTH ARMY CORPS,
March 14, 1863.

The other day, at Acquia Creek Landing, a soldier attempted to desert by putting off in a boat; a sergeant of a guard stationed there saw him and ordered him back; deserter didn't come; sergeant of the guard fired over his head and repeated his order; deserter laughed at him; sergeant fired again, hit deserter in a vital spot and he died shortly afterward. Some of the officers about there kicked up a row, and I believe put the sergeant in arrest. The affair came to

General Hooker's ears; he ordered the sergeant's release and personally wrote to him a very complimentary letter and promised him speedy promotion. These things take wonderfully well.

I am fully disposed to give General Hooker credit for every good thing he does; I believe him to be an active, hard-working man, and that he appreciates the very high position that he holds. I most earnestly hope that he will meet with every success in the coming campaign. I believe that the army was never in better condition in health and morale than it is now, very different from what it was a month ago. The signs of the times are encouraging; there doesn't seem to be so strong a desire on the part of the Government to interfere with army movements. Just let the draft be started and enforced, then we're ready for hard knocks.

* * *

HEADQUARTERS TWELFTH ARMY CORPS,
March 23, 1863.

I bought me a horse in a very unpremeditated way this afternoon. I was out riding and met a surgeon whom I know; he told me that he was going home for good, that he must sell his horse; I liked the animal's appearance very much, so asked permission to try him. After a short trial I made up my mind that if he would pass muster before our Chief Quartermaster, a great horse man, I would buy him. Colonel Hopkins, Quartermaster, advised me strongly to do so, and pronounced him sound and a very good beast; so after some haggling, I called him mine to the tune of one hundred and twenty-five dollars, saddle and bridle thrown in. I believe

I have a very good horse; he's a powerful, great, black
fellow, very spirited, and will be handsome with a little care.
He was taken from the rebels at the first Bull Run, and is
said to have belonged to the Black Horse Cavalry. I've been
thinking of buying for some time; it is not very satisfactory
riding government horses: it is very hard to get a very good
one, and I hate to ride an ordinary beast.

⚜ ⚜ ⚜

HEADQUARTERS TWELFTH ARMY CORPS,
April 5, 1863.

Again everything has the appearance of winter. Last
night a furious storm of wind, snow and hail set in, and continued till near noon to-day. It will melt very fast, of course,
but the roads, which before were nearly dry, will go back to
their former state of mud. I got caught in the storm last
night; I had been over to the cavalry with Tom Robeson;
when we came back, the wind, hail and dust were directly in
our faces and were perfectly blinding; the wind blew such a
gale that the horses could hardly breast up against it.

I wouldn't have believed, two months ago, that popular
feeling would be so unanimously for war. They have at last
waked up to the fact that we've got to fight these rebels till
we crush them, let it take one year or ten, and that there is
no peace now but in dishonor and eternal disgrace. Who
would have thought when the war broke out, that such
sentiments could have been publicly uttered in Baltimore
and Washington, as have been spoken at the late Union
meeting there!

HEADQUARTERS TWELFTH ARMY CORPS,
April 6, 1863.

I wish you could have seen the great military display there was near here yesterday. You probably have seen by the papers that President Abe is paying a visit to the army; he came down in the great snow-storm Saturday night. Well, yesterday was appointed for a grand review of all the cavalry and horse artillery in the army. All the Major-Generals and many of the Brigadiers with their staffs were invited to be present. Our cortege left these headquarters about half-past ten. We made a pretty good show by ourselves; there were five general officers, namely; Major-General Slocum, Brigadier-Generals Williams, Ruger, Knipe and Jackson, with their staffs and escorts, all in full fig. We rode about seven miles to the reviewing ground and got there just as the President, General Hooker and their large retinue arrived; the artillery fired the salute and the review commenced.

In the centre opposite the troops, looking sick and worn out, dressed in a plain black suit with the tallest of stove-pipe hats, was the President, seated on a fine horse with rich trimmings. On his right and left were Generals Hooker and Stoneman, and clustering around on all sides were Major and Brigadier-Generals too numerous to mention.

You know the story of a man who threw a bootjack out of a hotel window in Washington, last winter, and hit six briga-diers and a dog, and said, " It wasn't a good night for briga-diers, either." Yesterday was a good day for them. Who would have thought, five years ago, that such a sight as this would ever be possible in democratic, republican America. I doubt if any country has ever seen so large a collection of officers of high rank; there could not have been less than a thousand officers of all grades in the cavalcade, and now-a-days most every one dresses well; so you can imagine that such a crowd, well mounted on handsome horses with rich housings, was a gallant and gay sight. The cavalry was in two lines, each about two miles long; there were nearly ten thousand of them. I never have seen anything like such a number of horsemen together before. Generally they looked very well; the best regiments in appearance were the First and Second United States and the First Massachusetts and the First Rhode Island. There were four batteries of horse artillery, and the last one went by "flying." You know the term, "horse artillery," is given to those batteries where all the gunners are mounted; this enables them to keep up with the cavalry.

＊　＊　＊

HEADQUARTERS TWELFTH ARMY CORPS,
April 12, 1863.

This last has been a week of excitement to all of us in the army. I wrote about the great cavalry review on Monday; the following Wednesday we went over to the grand review of the Second, Third, Fifth and Sixth Corps. You have undoubtedly read in the papers better accounts of it than I can write, so I won't go into detail. It was a magnificent sight, I can tell you; there was the same brilliant cavalcade as I described at the cavalry review, — if anything, larger. The troops looked finely, better than I ever expected to see in our army. You can get some idea of the number of troops reviewed when I tell you that, for nearly two hours, they were passing steadily in solid column. From where we stood, we could see this moving mass for at least half a mile; it was a thrilling sight and one never to be forgotten. I felt proud of our Massachusetts regiments, for, as a rule, they were the best that passed, and most every one had a record that no one need be ashamed of.

Friday, the President, General Hooker, and train, came over to Stafford and reviewed our Corps and the Eleventh; this was another brilliant pageant. I believe we fully kept up the credit of the army. The old Second shone out, of course, "Excelsior," and was noticed and spoken of by a great many. After the show, Mr. and Mrs. Lincoln, General Hooker, and several other generals and officers with their staffs, came to our headquarters and we gave them a very good entertainment, cold meats, etc., etc.

After such an opportunity of seeing our army as I've had this last week, I cannot help comparing its present condition with that of the first army we saw, Patterson's: the last named a miserable mob of undisciplined, dirty men, but the Army of the Potomac a collection of as fine troops, I firmly believe, as there are in the world. I believe the day will come when it will be a proud thing for any one to say he belonged to it.

*   *

PROVOST MARSHAL'S OFFICE,
TWELFTH ARMY CORPS,
April 14, 1863.

Our army is beginning to move; yesterday, the cavalry started with a small infantry support. We are under orders and shall move probably to-morrow or next day. All extra clothing of the soldiers has been turned in, and all available room in knapsacks and haversacks has been filled with rations. My idea is something of this kind: that we are going up the Rappahannock at least as far as where the bridge on the Culpepper road was burned; that we shall cross there, then move forward a little; then that our right will be swung round, when the rebels will be obliged to abandon their fortifications and fight us on a fair field. If we win a victory. it will be a glorious one; at all events, we are going to give the enemy a harder fight than they have ever had before. I have been busy to-day making arrangements for a move. I think that I shall be able when the battle comes, to volunteer my services as aide to General Slocum; I hope so. It would give me a good chance to see the fight from various parts of the field; I feel sure he will make this corps do more than it has done yet. I have permission to send back my three companies when the regiment goes into action, so the Second will be able to give a good account of itself.

* * *

STAFFORD C. H., May 7, 1863.

I am going to give you, without any introduction, a history of this last campaign against Richmond by the army under the great Joe Hooker. I believe I have seen it and judged it fairly.

On Monday, April 27th, our corps broke camp early in the morning and marched to Hartwood Church, ten miles; there it went into camp for the night. The Eleventh and Fifth Corps also came up there and camped in our vicinity; next morning, we all moved and camped that night near Kelly's Ford. A pontoon bridge was thrown across and the

Eleventh was over before daylight Wednesday; the other corps followed rapidly and the advance began towards the Rapidan. The Eleventh and Twelfth marched on the road to Germana Ford, the Fifth on the road to Ely's Ford; all three of the corps were under command of General Slocum. I was detailed, the morning of the advance, as Aide to General Slocum, and another officer was made Acting Provost Marshal. All the companies of the Second Massachusetts were sent to the Regiment. We skirmished all the way to Germana Ford; there we met quite a determined resistance; our cavalry was drawn in and the Second Massachusetts and the Third Wisconsin sent forward to clear the way; they drove everything before them and, by their heavy fire, forced the rebels at the Ford to surrender (about one hundred officers and men). We lost in this skirmish about a dozen killed and wounded.

General Slocum now determined to cross the Rapidan, though there was no bridge and the ford was almost impassable. He sent the First and Third Brigade, (First Division, Twelfth Corps), through the water although it was more than waist deep, also five batteries of artillery, which took position on the other side of the river. A bridge was then constructed, and before daylight Thursday morning, the remainder of the Twelfth and Eleventh Corps were across the river. By eight o'clock, A. M., we were moving again. The rebels kept attacking us on our flank with cavalry and artillery, and any less bold officer than General Slocum would have halted his column and delayed the march; but he kept along steadily, detaching a small force at intervals to repel the enemy. I had the pleasure of superintending, at one of these skirmishes, having in charge the Twenty-ninth Pennsylvania Regiment; we drove the rebels before us for nearly a mile, almost capturing their artillery, taking a large number of prisoners. At about noon, we arrived at Chancellorsville, and found the Fifth Corps already there. We had a small cavalry skirmish, in which Colonel McVicars was killed with about a dozen of his men, but besides that, nothing of importance occurred that day: the troops were formed in line of battle, but were not attacked. Up to this time you see everything had gone well and success seemed certain.

Towards night, General Hooker arrived with his staff, and we heard of the crossing at the U. S. Ford of the Second, Third and First Corps. All the headquarters were in the vicinity of the Chancellor House, a large, fine brick mansion. General Hooker took supper with General Slocum; he didn't seem to be able to express his gratification at the success of General Slocum in bringing the three corps up so rapidly. Then, in the most extravagant, vehement terms, he went on to say how he had got the rebels, how he was going to crush them, annihilate them, etc.

The next morning at ten, the Fifth and Twelfth Corps advanced in order of battle on two parallel roads; we soon met the enemy and skirmished for about two miles, when they appeared in considerable force and the battle began. We were in a splendid position and were driving the enemy when an order came to General Slocum to retire his command to its former position. No one could believe that the order was genuine, but almost immediately, another of General Hooker's staff brought the same order again. Now, perhaps, you don't know that to retire an army in the face of an enemy when you are engaged, is one of the most difficult operations in war; this we had to do. I carried the order to General Geary to retire his division in echelon by brigades, and stayed with him till the movement was nearly completed. It was a delicate job; each brigade would successively bear the brunt of the enemy's attack. Before the last brigades of the Fifth and Twelfth Corps were in position, the enemy made a furious attack on the Chancellor House; luckily, we had considerable artillery concentrated there and they were driven back. The next attack was on our corps, but the enemy were severely repulsed. This about ended the fighting on Friday; we lost, I suppose, about five hundred men.

During the night, the men were kept at work digging trenches and throwing up breastworks of logs. Our headquarters were at Fairview, an open piece of ground rising into quite a crest in the centre. Skirmishing began at daylight next morning and continued without much result to either side, till afternoon, when the enemy began to move, in large force, towards our right, opposite General Howard, Eleventh Corps. This corps was in a fine position in intrenchments, with almost open country in front of them, the right resting on Hunting creek. At about four P M., the Third Corps, General Sickles, was moved out to the right of the Twelfth and advanced towards Fredericksburgh. The order then came to General Slocum that the enemy were in full retreat, and to advance his whole line to capture all he could of prisoners, wagons, etc. Our right, General Williams' Division, advanced without much trouble, driving the enemy before it, but the Second Division had hardly got out of the trenches before it was attacked with great determination, yet it steadily retained its position. At about five P M., a tremendous and unceasing musketry fire began in the direction of the Eleventh Corps. As it was necessary to know what was going on there in order to reg-

ulate the movements of the Twelfth Corps, General Slocum
and the rest of us rode for our lives towards this new scene
of action. What was our surprise when we found, that instead of a fight, it was a complete Bull Run rout. Men,
horses, mules, rebel prisoners, wagons, guns, etc., etc., were
coming down the road in terrible confusion, behind them an
unceasing roar of musketry. We rode until we got into a
mighty hot fire, and found that no one was attempting to
make a stand, but every one running for his life. Then General Slocum dispatched me to General Hooker to explain the
state of affairs, and three other staff officers to find General
Williams and order him back to his trenches with all haste.

I found General Hooker sitting alone on his horse in front
of the Chancellor House, and delivered my message; he merely
said, " Very good, sir." I rode back and found the Eleventh
Corps still surging up the road and still this terrible roar
behind them. Up to this time, the rebels had received no
check, but now troops began to march out on the plank road
and form across it, and Captain Best, Chief of Artillery of
our corps, had on his own responsibility gathered together
all the batteries he could get hold of, had put them in
position (forty-six guns in all) on Fairview, and had begun
firing at the rate of about one hundred guns a minute,
into the rebels. This, in my opinion, saved our army from
destruction. After delivering my message to General Hooker,
I went back and tried to find General Slocum, but it was now
after eight o'clock and I was unsuccessful in my search, so I
took hold and tried to rally some of the cowardly Dutchmen.
With the help of one cavalry orderly, I succeeded in forming
a good many of them on the left of the new line, but an un-
usually heavy volley coming, they broke and ran like sheep.

After this little episode, I again searched after the General. Towards ten, I found the rest of the staff, and soon after, we came across the General. At about eleven, the fighting stopped, but we were all hard at work getting the men of our corps into position. You see, while our First Division was advancing, the rebels had routed the Teutons and were now occupying our trenches. The Second and Third Brigades got into their former position, but the First made out only to cut through the rebels, losing a large part of its men and taking a position considerably in the rear of its former one. General Sickles fought his way through with the exception of one division and one battery, which were left out in front of our lines that night. The artillery men were hard at work all night, throwing up traverses to protect their guns, and about two in the morning we all lay down on the ground and slept until about four, when daylight began to appear. Our right was now formed by the Third, Fifth and First Corps, about five hundred yards in the rear of our first position. The rebels began the attack, as soon as there was light enough, from the left of our First Division to about the right of the Third Corps. General Birney's Division of the Third Corps was out in front of General Williams; his men behaved badly, and after a slight resistance, fell back into our lines, losing a battery.

The rebels now charged down our First Division, but were met with such a deadly fire that they were almost annihilated. Their second line was then sent in, but met the same fate, and their third and last line advanced. Our men now had fired more than forty rounds of cartridges and were getting exhausted. General Slocum sent almost every one of his staff officers to General Hooker, stating his position and begging for support; Hooker's answer was, "I can't make men or ammunition for General Slocum." Meantime, Sickles' Corps was holding its own on the right of ours, but it was rapidly getting into the same condition as the Twelfth. The rebels were driven back every time they advanced, and we were taking large numbers of prisoners and colors. All this time while our infantry was fighting so gallantly in front, our battery of forty-six guns was firing incessantly. The rebels had used no artillery till they captured the battery from Birney, when they turned that on us, making terrible destruction in General Geary's line. General Meade, Fifth Corps, now went to Hooker and entreated that he might be allowed to throw his corps on the rebel flank, but General Hooker said, "No, he was wanted in his own position." On his own responsibility, General Meade sent out one brigade, which passed out in rear of the enemy's right, recaptured a battery, three hundred of our men who were prisoners, and four hundred of the rebels, and took them safely back to their corps.

It was now after seven o'clock. Our men had fired their sixty rounds of cartridges and were still holding their position; everything that brave men could do, these men had done, but now nothing was left but to order them to fall back and give up their position to the enemy. This was done in good order and they marched off under a heavy fire to the rear of our batteries. The rebels, seeing us retreating, rushed forward their artillery and began a fearful fire. I found I could be useful to Captain Best, commanding our artillery, so I stayed with him. I never before saw anything so fine as the attack on that battery; the air was full of missiles, solid shot, shells, and musket balls. I saw one solid shot kill three horses and a man, another took a leg off one of the captains of the batteries. Lieutenant Crosby of the Fourth Artillery was shot through the heart with a musket ball: he was a particular friend of Bob Shaw and myself: he lived just long enough to say to Captain Best, "Tell father I die happy."

The rebels came up to the attack in solid masses and got within three hundred yards, but they were slaughtered by the hundreds by the case-shot and canister, and were driven back to the woods. Still not an infantry man was sent to the support of the guns. More than half the horses were killed or wounded; one caisson had blown up, another had been knocked to pieces: in ten minutes more, the guns would have been isolated. They, too, therefore, were ordered to retire, which they did without losing a gun. You see, now, our centre was broken, everything was being retired to our second line, the rebel artillery was in position, their line of battle steadily advancing across our old ground. This fire of the batteries was concentrated on the Chancellor House, Hooker's original headquarters, and it was torn almost to pieces by solid shot and was finally set on fire by a shell.

The army was now put in position in the second line: the centre was on a rising piece of ground and protected by a battery of forty or fifty guns. The Fifth Corps was on the right and was the last to fall back out of the woods and it was closely followed by the rebel masses, but these were met by such a tremendous artillery fire that they were actually rolled back into the woods. Our corps was ordered to support first the Third, afterwards the Second and Eleventh. Towards night the enemy made another desperate assault on our centre, but they were again repulsed. Our corps was now ordered to the extreme left to form behind the Eleventh. I believe that General Slocum remonstrated with General

Hooker so firmly that he finally got permission to put the Twelfth Corps on the extreme left and to have only one division of the Eleventh in the trenches on his right.

You can easily see that, if the enemy once forced our right or left, our communications would at once be cut and all possibility of retreat prevented. Late that night, we lay down close beside the Rappahannock. By three o'clock next morning, we were awakened by a heavy artillery fire and shells bursting over us. Our guns replied and kept at it for about an hour, when the enemy's batteries were silenced. We now mounted our horses and rode along the lines to look at our position; we found that it was a very strong one and capable of being made very much more so.

We found that the sharpshooters were getting altogether too attentive to our party, so we moved back to our line and had hardly turned away, when a sergeant was shot dead almost on the spot where the general had been standing. All that day, our men were hard at work throwing up breastworks, cutting abattis, etc. No attack was made on us, but throughout that day and night, we heard Sedgwick fighting in the direction of Fredericksburgh.

Tuesday morning, I knew by appearances that a retreat was to be effected, as a large part of the artillery, all the ambulances, etc., were removed across the river, although the men were kept at work making line after line of trenches and breastworks. Just before dark, the order of retreat came, the Fifth and Twelfth Corps being the last to cross. About four o'clock that afternoon it began to rain in torrents. There were originally three pontoon bridges, but before most of the crossing had been effected, the river became so swollen that one of the bridges had to be taken up to piece out the other two; this caused a great delay. At about twelve, I was sent down to the ford to examine into the condition of things; it was a terrible night, the wind blowing a gale and the rain pouring, the road for a mile full of artillery. I found, at the bridge, that not a thing was moving, and learned from General Patrick that the order for retreat had been suspended and everything was to move back to its former position. This order came, remember, when half of the artillery was on the north side of the Rappahannock, the soldiers without a ration and the supply trains ten miles the other side of the river. I ran my horse back to headquarters and made my report; the telegraph was down between U. S. Ford and Falmouth, *where General Hooker was*. General Slocum wrote a dispatch, saying, that unless the movement was continued, our army would have to be surrendered within twenty-four hours; this was sent by an orderly who was ordered to kill his horse carrying it. Then to prepare for the worst, General Slocum sent one of his aides and myself back to the Ford to get our artillery ready to move back into position, that our corps might, at least, be ready to make a desperate fight in the morning; but at about two-thirty A. M., the messenger returned from General Hooker with orders for the movement to continue.

At about five, one of our divisions began to cross. The two or three succeeding hours were the most anxious I ever passed in my life. A large part of our army was massed on the south side of the river, only two bridges for the whole of it to cross, the river full to the edge of its banks; a very little extra strain would have carried away the upper bridge, and this would have swept away the lower one and all retreat would have been cut off. The rebel artillery began to fire on our troops and bridges, but was silenced by our guns; we had sixty in position on the north side.

It soon became evident that the enemy were not in force in our vicinity, but for all that, it was one of the happiest moments of my life when I saw the last of our corps over the bridge. We all started then for Stafford C. H., where our corps was ordered to its old camp. We arrived at our old headquarters at about two P M., and found, to our joy, that our wagons had arrived and tents were being pitched. It was not until after we were in comfortable quarters that the terrible fatigue of the last ten days began to tell on us. Since we had left Stafford, we had been without wagons or blankets, with nothing to eat except pork and hard bread, and half the time not even that, and we had averaged each day at least twelve or sixteen hours in the saddle. The moment we touched a seat, we sunk into the most profound sleep and stayed in this condition for several hours. It may seem strange to you that I speak of being happy to get back into our old quarters, but you must remember that we had been through danger and hardship for ten days and had met with constant disappointment and were now safe back again where we were going to have sleep, rest, and food.

Now, let us see what this campaign shows. It seems to me that the plan was a very good one, with the exception of separating Sedgwick with thirty thousand men from the army, and that it was carried out with great success till General Hooker arrived at Chancellorsville. The next thing shown is that the commander of our army gained his position by merely brag and blow, and that when the time came to show himself, he was found without the qualities necessary for a general. If another battle had been fought on Monday, it would have been by the combined corps commanders, and the battle would have been won.

I doubt if, ever in the history of this war, another chance will be given us to fight the enemy with such odds in our favor as we had last Sunday, and that chance has been worse than lost to us. I don't believe any men ever fought better than our Twelfth Corps, especially the First Division; for two hours, they held their ground without any support, against the repeated assaults of the enemy; they fired their sixty rounds of cartridges and held their line with empty muskets till ordered to fall back. The old Second, of course, did splendidly, and lost heavily, twenty-two killed, one hundred and four wounded, ten missing; my company had five killed and eleven wounded. Lieutenant Fitzgerald was killed, Coggswell, Grafton, Perkins, and Powers, wounded. George Thompson had a narrow escape; a grape shot tore one leg of his trousers and his coat almost off and grazed his leg. Our colors got thirty new holes in them and the staff (the third one), was smashed to pieces.*

You cannot imagine the amount of admiration I have for General Slocum, for the gallant way in which he conducted himself throughout the campaign, and his skillful management of his command; then besides all that, we have been so together, that he has seemed almost like my old friends in the regiment.

I have written in this letter a pretty full account of the operations as I have seen them, and I don't believe any one has had a better chance, for during the fighting, I was at

---

* Actual loss: 31 killed and mortally wounded, 91 wounded, 7 prisoners. Total loss, 129.

different times at every part of our lines, and in communication with General Hooker and other generals.

Our staff casualties were as follows: — Lieutenant Tracy, badly wounded in right arm, his horse shot in four places; one of our orderlies shot and two more horses. I feel thankful to have come out unharmed from so much danger. Tracy was carrying an order to General Williams, when he was hit; somehow, he got outside our lines and was ordered to surrender; he said he thought he wouldn't, turned his horse and ran for it, while the rebels put two volleys after him.

I telegraphed, last Monday, that I was all right; I hope you received the message.

✿ ✿ ✿

HEADQUARTERS TWELFTH CORPS,
June 12, 1863.

The picked regiments of the different corps were sent off with the cavalry Saturday evening on an expedition; of course, this took in the Third Wisconsin and the Second Massachusetts. I see by the papers that there has been a fight and that our regiments have lost several men each.

✿ ✿ ✿

NEAR LEESBURG, June 22, 1863.

I wrote a short note yesterday to let you know my whereabouts and relieve any anxiety you might feel for me; to-day I'll try to give you a few particulars of our movements.*

---

* The writer had been promoted to be Major of his regiment but had not yet received his commission.

Friday, the 12th, I left headquarters, ease and luxury. The regiment was still away with the cavalry. However, the camp was standing and about sixty men and two or three officers were there who had been left behind for various reasons, so I had a small command.

That night, orders came to march at daylight. We moved back about three miles towards Acquia Creek, stayed there through the day, and at night started forward again and marched till eight the following morning, halting this side of Dumfries. Sunday, we rested all day while the train of our corps and the Sixth passed by. Monday, we started at three in the morning and marched twenty-three miles under a burning sun to Fairfax C. H., getting into camp about ten P M. This was a really terrible march; the day was very hot and a great part of the time we were marching side by side with a column of wagons, which raised a dust that was almost choking. Next morning, Tuesday, about eight, the Second Massachusetts and Third Wisconsin made their appearance from their cavalry excursion : they marched into camp covered with dust and dirt, but looking soldierly as ever. All the regiments of the corps that were near by turned out to have a look at them and give them very hearty greetings, for the two old regiments are now pretty well known in the corps.

I had a very pleasant time hearing the accounts of the fight at Beverly Ford; all seemed to think that if they had to fight cavalry only till the end of the war, they would have a very jolly time. Whenever our infantry skirmishers made their appearance, the cavalry left in a hurry, showing a great respect for our Enfields.

A company of the Second and one of the Third Wisconsin, made an attack on about two hundred of the enemy's cavalry who were dismounted and lying behind a stone wall firing their carbines; our men, not numbering more than forty in all, fired one volley, then made a rush, capturing over twenty and finding, at least, as many killed by their shots. Wednesday morning, we marched again to near Drainsville. Thursday, we marched again, reaching Leesburg towards night. All of the corps, except our regiment and the Third Wisconsin with a battery of artillery, remained east of the town; we kept on a mile farther and occupied a fort and strong position on one of the Katoctin Hills.

We are still in this same position, how long to remain, no one here knows. Our army lies stretched away for a number of miles towards Thoroughfare Gap, the Eleventh Corps occupying an important position on our right, its flank touching the Potomac.

We can only surmise whether Lee will attack us here or not; he is moving somewhere in our front but not very near. We have at last had a severe rain storm and the weather is more comfortable. It hailed for about an hour very severely; the hailstones were, at least, as large as rifle bullets; I was riding at the time and could hardly force my horse against the storm; he would rear and kick, and didn't seem to understand at all what was going on.

The battle that I spoke of yesterday proves to have been quite a success for us; we drove the rebels three miles and captured three guns and some prisoners. Our wagon camp is on the field where Ball's Bluff was fought. I am in command of the regiment now, Major Mudge being on Court Martial. I don't see anything of my commission yet.

* * *

BATTLEFIELD NEAR GETTYSBURG,
July 4, 1863.

I have again passed safely through a terrible battle of three days. The regiment has lost terribly: two officers killed, Major Mudge and Lieutenant Stone, Captains Robeson and Fox mortally wounded, six other officers wounded, ninety-five men wounded, thirty killed.*

The battle isn't over, but I hope we've seen the worst of it.

   * * *

NEAR WILLIAMSPORT, July 13, 1863.

We are now in line of battle fortifying our position. The enemy is in front; I don't think Meade is at all anxious to make the attack, for we don't believe as the papers do, that we have a demoralized army to fight, but one nearly as strong as we are, in a good position for defence: still I think there will be a fight before they get over the river.

The first chance I have, I will write you an account of our part of the battle of Gettysburg. It was a fierce fight: we made one charge which was the bravest thing I ever saw. It was in this that Colonel Mudge and most of the officers and men were hit. There are only four of the old officers left in the field and line of this regiment now, Coggswell, myself, Francis and Brown; of twelve officers who have been killed, eleven came out with the regiment.

I received a very handsome letter from General Andrews yesterday in which he offered me the colonelcy of a colored

---

* Actual loss: 45 killed and mortally wounded, 90 wounded, 5 prisoners. Total loss, 140.

regiment. He is to have the organization and command of a Corps d'Afrique consisting of twenty regiments of infantry, one regiment of cavalry and four batteries. Under the circumstances I shall refuse, but I consider it a great honor, coming from him.

⚘ ⚘ ⚘

PLEASANT VALLEY, July 17, 1863.

As usual it is raining to-day, for I think it has rained almost every day for three weeks, more or less, so I am going to write to you some account of our last campaign.

I believe my last letter describing our progress was from Leesburg. From there, by a succession of long marches, we went to Littleton; here we had a little excitement caused by a cavalry skirmish just in front of us, but we were not called on to do anything. The first of July, we moved towards Gettysburg to a small place called "Two Taverns;" there we began to hear cannonading in our front, and in the afternoon, we were ordered forward to support the force which was engaged. We were put into position but did nothing that afternoon and lay on our arms that night. We heard, that night, of the death of General Reynolds. Next morning, we changed position again. It was a fine place in a beautiful, open wood. About three o'clock in the afternoon, the battle began on the left; the musketry became fearful; it was a terribly anxious time with us, more so, I think, than if we were actually engaged. Every eye was turned in the direction of the firing, fearful lest at any moment we might see our troops coming back through the woods. Happily, we saw no such sight, but we did see, with pleasure, the old Fifth Corps going up to support the gallant troops who were fighting.

About half-past six our turn came ; we, too, were ordered from the right to the left ; only one brigade of our corps was left in the breastwork we had constructed. We arrived on the battle-ground, but before we got there the enemy had been repulsed severely, so back we started to our old position. It was now between eight and nine o'clock, clear and moonlight. While we had been away, Mr. Johnny Reb had come with a strong force and got our breastworks ; the brigade left behind had had a severe fight and had partially driven the enemy out, but darkness came on, and the fight stopped. Our brigade was ordered to advance cautiously and get into the breastwork. We crept quietly along ; not a word was spoken nor an unnecessary noise made. All the regiments had got into their former positions without trouble except the Second. We were just marching out of the woods into a little open meadow in the clear moonlight, when our skirmishers brought in a rebel prisoner : this showed our proximity to the enemy, so we changed our front and made preparation to fight for our position.

The skirmishers were reinforced and again advanced. In five minutes we had captured a captain and twenty-two other prisoners ; still not a shot was fired. These men appeared to be stragglers who had lost their command. We began to think that, after all, perhaps there was no force in front of us ; so the regiment was again ordered to advance. Colonel Mudge put me in charge of the line of skirmishers : the meadow was narrow, and we soon entered the woods again, where it was quite dark. We crawled along cautiously and quietly, till we began to hear a confused sound of talking in front of us : we now halted. Not daring to do anything more without being certain what troops they were (for we knew

our Second Division was trying to work down towards us), I
ordered two men to go forward and ask them. They walked
up to within a few paces of the line ; one of them said,
" Boys, what regiment do you belong to ? " The reply was,
" Twenty-third."   " Twenty-third what ? "   " Twenty-third
Virginia."   Then some one cried out, " Why, they are
Yanks." and seized one of my men ; the other bolted back
to me and escaped. I sent word back to Colonel Mudge
what I had discovered, and he withdrew the regiment beyond
the meadow.

The behavior of the rebels puzzled me ; I couldn't make
out what they were up to ; they were certainly there within
talking distance, but they seemed in confusion as if they
didn't know their ground and showed no inclination to fire
or advance upon us. I now resolved on a bold stroke. The
men were ordered to advance with some noise ; almost instantly the challenge rang out from the rebel lines, " Who
comes there ? " Captain Fox had received his instructions
and called out in answer, " Surrender ! Come into our lines."
The impudence of this request must have struck the rebel
commander, for his answer was, in a loud voice, " Battalion,
ready, aim, fire ! " A heavy volley was fired, but luckily the
ground where we were was low and the men scattered at
intervals, so that not much damage was done, only three men
being wounded.

They followed this up by a rush, and we ran for it ;
they followed only a short distance, but I made up my
mind that we had had enough skylarking for one night, and
returned therefore with all the men to the regiment, bringing
three more rebel prisoners. It was now between twelve and
one ; we lay down with arms in our hands, to get a little rest.

At the first streak of daylight, we were waked up by heavy musketry firing in the direction of our second division, the enemy being in force between our two divisions.

Captain Robeson with his company were out as skirmishers in front of our line; they became engaged as soon as it was light enough to see anything. At about half-past five, Colonel Colgrove gave the order to Colonel Mudge to advance his regiment and charge the woods opposite us. Colonel Mudge gave the order, "Forward;" the men jumped over the breastworks and rushed forward with a splendid cheer. We had to cross the little meadow I have spoken of; here was where we suffered so heavily; the enemy was in the woods and we in the open. We reached the opposite woods and commenced firing at the shortest range I have ever seen two lines engaged at. We fought the rebs before us for about ten minutes; then I learned that Colonel Mudge had been hit and that I was in command; I was on the left at the time. I went up to the right to see how things were getting along there; I found, to my surprise, that the regiment that had advanced with us was not on our right and the enemy were working round that way trying to get in our rear. I ordered a change of position to the rear, throwing our right back a little, which put the rebels in as bad a place as they thought to put us and we drove them back again. We stayed here till all our ammunition was expended, when we were ordered back by Colonel Colgrove.

It was a sad thing calling the rolls and looking at the vacant places of so many officers; our only consolation was that they had done their duty nobly in as brave an action as ever a regiment went into. Five color bearers were shot down, one after another, three were killed, two badly wounded, but the tattered flag never tonched the ground. The third man who seized it jumped on to a rock in advance of the regiment and waved it triumphantly in the air, but the brave action cost him his life; he fell dead beside the others.

[During the interval between the next letter and the preceding one, the writer was on detached service engaged in bringing conscripts from Long Island, Boston Harbor, to the Army of the Potomac.]

♪ ♪ ♪

WASHINGTON, October 2, 1863.

I arrived here this morning. The Twelfth and Eleventh Corps have gone to Nashville under command of General Hooker, probably to relieve some troops which have gone forward to Chattanooga. General Slocum's resignation was not accepted and he has gone in command of the corps.

I shall probably leave here at six thirty, P M., and travel all night.

♪ ♪ ♪

WARTRACE, TENN., October 15, 1863.

You see where I am at once, but before telling you how it came about I will go back a little. My last letter was from Nashville, dated the 8th. The next day, Friday, the railroad was reopened. I took a train about two, P M., and started to find my regiment. At Murfreesboro, where we arrived about five, I came across General Williams and staff, who told me that the Second was at Christiana, about ten miles further on. It was after dark before we got there, but the regiment was near at hand, and I soon found myself in camp again, much to the surprise of the Colonel and other officers, who welcomed me with open arms. That night, I returned to first principles, hard bread and coffee out of a tin cup, sleeping under a shelter tent with no covering but my rubber cloak. We were roused up before daylight in the morning, to start on a long march towards Tullahoma. I started on foot, but one of General Ruger's aides soon after furnished me with an ancient Government animal which had been turned away as unfit for service and was caparisoned with a saddle and bridle of the country, in a very lamentable state of decay; however, this was better than walking, so I mounted him, not without serious misgivings that I should suddenly be lowered to the ground by reason of his knees giving way under him. This did occur once when I urged him to a trot, but I stuck manfully to my seat and made him rise with me.

Colonel Cogswell's charger was also of the Rosinante pattern, and being white showed his "points" to a still greater advantage. Thus mounted, you can imagine we did not make a very imposing appearance. We marched till eight P M., accomplishing about twenty-four miles, and camped in a corn field. We were off again before daylight the next morning, and marched fifteen miles to within four miles of Deckard, camping on the banks of the Elk Run, over which there is an important railroad bridge. For the present, this bridge is to be guarded by our regiment, the Third Wisconsin. One Hundred and Seventh New York, First Tennessee Black Regiment, a battery and a few other detachments. Our camp was right alongside of the "darks." Their Colonel and Lieutenant Colonel came over to see us and proved to be very pleasant gentlemen; they were profuse in their offers of hospitality. This is one very noticeable characteristic of western officers; no matter how rough they are, or how much they blow for their army, etc., they are perfectly liberal in their ideas and are as hospitable as men can be, offering us horses, rations or anything else we want. They brag a great deal of the fighting and marching of the Army of the Cumberland, and pretend to think that the Army of the Potomac has done very little of either, but the western regiments in our corps give these gentlemen very emphatic information as to our fights and losses, and they seldom have as good stories to tell in return. They acknowledge to have been very severely handled both at Stone River and Chickamauga, although at the former place, the enemy retreated and we claimed a victory.

To go back to the black regiment. The night of our arrival, we all went over to see dress parade. We were told beforehand by Colonel Thompson (formerly of General Rosecrans' staff) that his men had not been in camp quite a month and had not yet been drilled on account of the heavy amount of picket duty, so we went prepared to excuse a great deal. I was very agreeably surprised by the whole appearance of the regiment : the men had a soldierly bearing, marched well, and stood in line better than nine-tenths of the white regiments I have seen. I didn't have an opportunity, myself, but the Colonel and Major both visited their picket line, and said that they never saw sentinels do their duty better. These men are nearly all of the blackest description, and very ignorant.

All our privates went over to see their parade. I would not want any severer critics. During the whole ceremony I saw no sneering or attempt to laugh, and after it was all over and the companies were marching off, our men applauded by a very hearty clapping. I looked upon this as a very strong indication of what the general feeling would be among our troops.

Monday morning, I received a telegram ordering me to report at corps headquarters at Wartrace. I was very much surprised at receiving it, as General Slocum had given me no intimation of it at Nashville. I felt sorry to leave the regiment so soon again ; but, of course, there were some reasons that made me glad to get to headquarters. I received that night the written order appointing me Provost Marshal and acting Assistant Adjutant General of the Twelfth Corps.

❧ ❧ ❧

WARTRACE, TENN., October 23, 1863.

We had just got comfortably settled down at this place when, yesterday, orders came to General Slocum to concentrate his corps as soon as possible at Bridgeport. The movement has commenced, and we shall probably break camp to-morrow. The change in commanders has, of course, been an important topic with us for the last few days. A man takes a great responsibility on his shoulders now, when he accepts the command of an army. We are fortunate in having as good a man as Thomas for the successor of Rosecrans. There is a great chance to speculate on the coming campaign.

We have rumors that two corps are moving east on the Memphis and Charleston R. R. This force, with the Twelfth and Eleventh Corps and Burnside's army, if concentrated at Chattanooga, would undoubtedly be large enough to give battle to Bragg, with a more than even chance of success. But the risk of having communication cut off is very great if our corps is entirely removed from the railroad ; it leaves about one hundred and twenty miles of road almost without a guard, and there is a succession of high trestle-work bridges all the way from Nashville to Bridgeport. At this present moment there is a band of some eight hundred guerrilla cavalry within twenty-five miles of this place, lying in wait for any opportunities they may have to destroy property. A strong force of cavalry could, within three days of our departure, stop this road from running for weeks. Still, I suppose that we have the chance of fighting Bragg before he can take advantage of this. Our worst enemy now is the weather. It has rained almost every day for the last ten days, and is very cold and disagreeable ; the roads, of course, are fearfully muddy; they are quite equal to Virginia roads. I have great confidence in General Thomas. General Slocum knew him well before the war, and has the highest kind of opinion of him ; he says he is as high-minded, noble, and kind-hearted a man as ever lived; that he has always opposed all kinds of humbug, and has never allowed any newspaper reporters about his corps, for which reason he hasn't enjoyed the brilliant reputation of a certain stripe of officers. He has really fine qualities, and I hope will be allowed to keep command.

⚜ ⚜ ⚜

WARTRACE, TENN., October 28, 1863.

When I wrote you last, I thought we were off immediately for the front, but the following day brought a great many changes of orders, the final ones being that General Slocum, with one division, should remain on the railroad, and that the other division should concentrate at Bridgeport, to march from there to Chattanooga.

Although we are very pleasantly situated here and are living very comfortably, I should very much prefer to be with the main army at the front. Rumor says that Buell is to be Grant's chief of staff. I hope this may be so ; I don't think that he has ever been justly appreciated. Old officers of the regular army say that Buell is the abler man of the two. Of course, now that Rosecrans is down, every cur has to have his snarl and bite at him. The *Washington Chronicle* has indulged in one of its characteristic articles about him. In some degree, I think he has brought it upon himself : he was before the public a great deal in the newspapers while he was in command of the Army of the Cumberland, and very often made public speeches and wrote public letters.

There is no use for a general to try and get popularity by anything except his acts ; newspaper talk does very well for a time, but it does not last or produce any impression on sensible men. Every one knows, nowadays, that he can get a puff by entertaining a correspondent well, and that the latter will flatter his vanity by praising his military ability. The men who stand best to-day with the army have hardly ever had their names in print except in public documents, like Sedgwick, Sykes, Hancock and their class.

*　*　*

NOTES FROM A JOURNAL.

When we first came to this place, General Slocum received a telegram from headquarters which said that if we needed any scouting or important secret service done, we had better use a certain John Douglas, who was very faithful and efficient. The General told me he wanted me to take charge of everything in the scouting department, and that I had better see Douglas as soon as possible. At this point, it is very necessary to depend on scouts and citizens, as our force is very small and we are entirely without cavalry, so I sent for Douglas and he came to see me the next morning.

I was very much struck by his appearance; he was the first man who came up at all to my idea of what a scout should be like. He is a man about fifty years old, I should think, medium size and a little bent over, but with a very tough, hard looking frame; his striking features, though, are his eyes; they are jet black and piercing in their expression, with a restless, eager look, as if he was always expecting to see the rifle of an enemy sticking out from behind a tree or bush; his eyebrows are also black, but his hair has turned gray with age. His walk was very peculiar, and was exactly like that described of Leather-stocking in the "Deerslayer," a sort of gait which, without seeming to be much exertion, was equal to what we call a dog trot. He made me think of all the old backwoods heroes I had ever read of, from Daniel Boone down.

I found that he had papers from Rosecrans, Burnside, Dupont and several others, all testifying to his marked ability and energy, and his entire knowledge of every part of Tennessee and northern Georgia, and Alabama. I talked with him some time and found that he was very intelligent and well informed.

A few days after my first interview with Douglas, I received a telegram from Murfreesboro stating that they had certain information that a band of six or eight hundred guerrillas were in the neighborhood of McMinnville. I sent for Douglas and told him I wanted to know the truth of the story. He didn't stay five minutes after I had told him the rumor; this was about seven o'clock in the evening. The next afternoon, about three o'clock, he made his appearance and said the story was true; since he left me, he had ridden nearly seventy miles to within three or four miles of the guerrilla camp. The next day we were told by some citizens that this cavalry was supported by infantry, and that it was the advance of a portion of Bragg's army. We didn't believe this at all; still I was anxious to find out just what the force was. I sent Douglas out again, telling him to find out every particular before he came back. He was gone two days, and on his return, he said he had spent several hours inside the enemy's camp; his information proved that we had nothing at all to fear from them except depredations. I asked him how he got inside their lines; he said that the picket he passed was a very green-looking countryman; that when he approached, he was ordered to halt; he rode up to the picket and said he was a bearer of dispatches to the commanding officer. " Who is the commanding officer ? " said the sentinel. " That is nothing to do with your instructions, and you will get into difficulty if you don't let me pass." The sentinel passed him, and he went inside and talked with the men and officers and saw the commanders. There was nothing remarkable in this, but a man discovered as a spy by these guerrillas would be hung or have his throat cut five minutes after he was caught.

The pay Douglas gets as chief of scouts of this vicinity is only three dollars per day, very small compensation for the risk. He has told me a number of stories of the sufferings of East Tennesseeans; they are equal to any of Brownlow's; he says there is no exaggeration in the latter's statements.

He told me of one young lady who lived with her mother near Knoxville, whose brothers and father were strong Unionists. They had hidden away among the mountains. He described her as a very refined, well educated young woman. One day, a party of guerrillas came to her house and took her and her mother out in the woods and tied them to a tree; they then asked them to tell where their men relations were hidden; they refused to tell them; these brutes gave them each a terrible whipping, but they still refused to give them any information. These chivalric gentlemen then put nooses round their necks, untied them and threatened them with instant hanging if they didn't tell what they required. The young girl told them they might be able to torture her more than she could bear, but before she would say one word that would compromise her father or brothers, she would bite off her tongue and spit it in their rebel faces.

They raised them off the ground three times, nearly killing them. Afterwards, this same girl became a spy for our cavalry and led them on several successful expeditions. Douglas was on one of them, and said that during a fight that occurred, she insisted on staying under the heaviest of the fire. She used sometimes to go inside the rebel lines and act as nurse in one of the rebel hospitals; after she had got all the information that she could, she would return inside our lines and tell what she had found out.

Yesterday there was very near being a terrible accident on the railroad, about fifty miles from here, in amongst the mountains. Some infernal guerrillas put a species of torpedo underneath a rail, just before the passenger train from Nashville was due. Fortunately a locomotive came along just before it and set the machine off; the explosion was tremendous ; the engine and tender were blown to pieces ; railroad ties and rails were blown as high as the tops of trees; the engineer was thrown twenty or thirty feet and severely injured. If it had not been for this locomotive, probably hundreds of men would have been killed and wounded, as the cars go crowded with officers and soldiers. The perpetrator of this outrage, of course, could not be discovered, but a man living near by seemed to be implicated, and his house and barn were burnt.

They are very summary in dealing with guerrillas in this country when they catch them. There is one despatch from General Crook to Rosecrans on record to this effect: that he (Crook) fell in with a party of guerrillas, twenty in number; that in the fight, twelve of them were killed and the rest were taken prisoners. He regrets to state that on the march to camp, the eight were so unfortunate as to fall off a log and break their necks.

*　*　*

TULLAHOMA, TENN., November 22, 1863.

We have been moving about so much lately that I have omitted to write my usual quota of letters. A little more than a week ago, General Slocum received orders to remove his headquarters to Murfreesboro; we arrived there about a week ago Friday, and established ourselves in Rosecrans' old headquarters, the residence of a rebel congressman. Before the war, it must have been a very elegant house, and even as we found it, stripped as it was of all furniture, it seemed quite magnificent to us after living in tents. My room had been the front drawing room and was still decorated by a white marble mantlepiece and bronze chandelier. Every room in the house had a fine, open fireplace in it.

We lived here very comfortably till last Monday, when General Slocum was ordered to Tullahoma on account of a new disposition of troops along the road. We left Murfreesboro Wednesday morning; that same morning Colonel Rogers started home on a sick leave, so that I became acting Assistant Adjutant General of the corps for the time being. The day was a perfect one, and both ourselves and horses felt in fine spirits for a march. Our intention was to ride to Shelbyville that day, about twenty miles. We passed through some of the finest farming country in middle Tennessee, and had a fine chance to see and enjoy it. Much of the land had been used for raising cotton, and occasionally we would meet a wagon-load of this valuable article on its way to Nashville. I don't know when I've enjoyed a ride so much as I did the one that day. We arrived in Shelbyville about sunset. This town is the second in size in Tennessee, and has been a very pretty place, almost like a Northern one; it has been the stronghold of the Unionists of the State. During Wheeler's raid the place was entered by the rebels, and every store and many of the houses were stripped of every article of value.

A gentleman named Ramsay invited the General and myself to stop at his house; we accepted the invitation and were treated with great hospitality. Our host was one of the leading Union men of the county, and we have since learned that it was in a great measure owing to him that the neighborhood had been kept so loyal. The county voted against secession by a very large majority. We left Shelbyville about eleven o'clock the next morning. Our ride that day was through a much wilder country than we had passed through on the day preceding : much of the road was nothing more than a cart-path through the woods, but this was very favorable for horseback riding, and we got along pretty fast. General Slocum came near meeting with a severe accident that afternoon. We were galloping along quite fast when his horse, a large, heavy animal, struck a bad place in the road and fell forward upon his knees ; before he could be recovered he rolled over on his side, pinning the General's leg to the ground. We all sprang from our horses, and, after some little struggling on the part of the horse, the General was extricated from his dangerous position. We all thought his leg was broken, for he looked deadly pale, but he relieved our anxiety by saying that he was all right, and after lying down a few minutes, he mounted his other horse and we rode on again. Tullahoma was reached about six P M., after a ride of twenty-three or four miles.

❦ ❦ ❦

TULLAHOMA, TENN., November 28, 1863.

We are in the midst of exciting news from the front, yet we have had no particulars. It is evident, however, that we have taken several thousand prisoners and a large quantity of artillery.*

Since the fight at Wauhatchie, there has been no slurring of the Army of the Potomac men. That little affair was a great thing for us. By our own and rebel accounts, there

* The battles of Missionary Ridge and Lookout Mountain.

is no doubt that our men fought most gallantly there against superior numbers of their old antagonists.

Every train that comes from the South brings a load of prisoners or wounded men, and rumors that fighting is still going on at the front. It seems to me, now, for the first time since the war began, that the rebellion is nearly crushed. They have not met with any very decisive success for nearly six months, and are now contracted into the smallest territory they have ever occupied.

Atlanta is our important point now ; get that, and we have again cut the Confederacy in two, and in a vital place. What a glorious thing it would be if we could wind up this rebellion before our original three years are out! It would exceed all my expectations to do this.

Thanksgiving Day was a very pleasant one, warm and bright as May. I took an escort of half a dozen cavalry and rode down to the regiment, which is about ten miles from here. I found them camped very comfortably just outside strong earthworks built to command the railroad bridge over the Elk river. Colonel Coggswell is in command of the post and has a battery in addition to his regiment. He has made himself very strong, and could defend the place against a large force.

I took a very quiet dinner with the field and staff. Of course we could not help thinking of our other Thanksgiving Days in the regiment, and it brought up many sad memories. At our first dinner at Seneca, Maryland, all our old officers were present ; last year there had been many changes, but there were still left a goodly number of the old stock, and we were knit closer together by our losses. This year I couldn't help a feeling of desolation as I remembered that, of all my friends in the regiment, very few were left. How little I thought, when we left Camp Andrews, that we should have such a sad experience!

In looking over his trunks for a photograph, Colonel Coggswell found a letter that had come for me while I was in Massachusetts; he gave it to me, and I found the address was in Bob Shaw's writing. You can imagine how glad I was to get it. I always thought it a little strange that he had not answered my last letter. I opened it the first chance I got. It was mostly a description of his movements to Darien and other places: but at the close he spoke in a very feeling way of our friendship and intimacy, and of his happiness since his marriage. It was written on the 3rd of July; in it he asked to be remembered to Robeson, Mudge, and Tom Fox; little did he think that, at the moment he wrote, one of them was lying dead on the field of battle, and the other two suffering with mortal wounds.

The men of the regiment had a very pleasant day; they had plenty of geese and turkeys for dinner, and in the evening the brigade band came down from Tullahoma, and gave them some music. I am glad that our men have each been able to keep this day somewhat as if they had been at home.

I stayed next morning and saw guard mounting done as it is done nowhere else, and then rode back here again.

TULLAHOMA, TENN.. December 24, 1863.

In my last letter, I spoke of having something important to write in a day or two; I referred to the very matter that you speak of in your letter, the re-enlistment of the old regiment. I have always been very earnest about it, but little was done in the matter till quite lately. Last Saturday night, General Ruger came over to headquarters and told us that the Third Wisconsin was busy re-enlisting and meant to get home during the holidays.

The next morning, I wrote as stirring a letter as I could to Colonel Coggswell; it had the effect to bring him to head-quarters that same afternoon. We consulted together for some time; I found that he was very enthusiastic and quite sanguine about the success of the movement, and that he spoke the sentiments of nearly all the officers of the regiment. The next day the colonel made a speech to the men and a good start was made, nearly one hundred putting their names down. On Tuesday, I went over to the camp; I found that some companies had done nobly, having already more than filled their quota (that is, more than three-quarters); others were hanging back. My old company hadn't made much of a start. I made them a little speech at "tattoo," and per-suaded some half-a-dozen to face the music again. So far, we have got about a hundred and fifty names, that is, a little more than half the requisite number.

Colonel Coggswell writes me to-night that everything is going on well, so that I've strong hopes of ultimate success, but I shall not give way to any excitement about it at present.

The spirit with which the line officers have gone into this thing is most noble. There's that young Crowninshield, with three bullet holes in his body, who is the most active of any of them, and has secured a great part of his company. One thing is sure — the bounty money is having very little to do with this re-enlistment; I don't think one man in ten thinks of it as a consideration ; the going home is what moves them. These old fellows who have been knocking about, and have been shot at for the last three years, may not have much care for money now, but they all show that they have not forgotten their homes and families. I tell you, if they do go in again, it will show what splendid stuff they are made of, and the regiment should gain more honor and credit for this than for any other act in its history.

You can easily imagine that it takes some inducement a good deal stronger than money to get soldiers in the ranks to exchange comfortable homes and firesides for the hard knocks and dangers of a campaign.

It is rather exciting to think of marching through Boston with our drum corps and old flag riddled with bullet holes.*

⁂

TULLAHOMA, TENN., March 24, 1864.

As I was sitting here writing this evening, a despatch for the General came into the office, which has brightened me up amazingly and put quite a new aspect upon the face of affairs. It was, in effect, that as soon as certain blockhouses were completed along the road, they would be occupied by small garrisons ; the rest of the corps, with the exception of garrisons at Nashville and Murfreesboro, would go under General Slocum to the front. Isn't this glorious news ? Of course, we can't tell yet whether we are going to the actual front of the army, yet it is certain we are going to have a chance.

---

*A sufficient number of the regiment re-enlisted to secure a furlough, and it returned to Boston in a body with all of its officers.

TULLAHOMA, TENN.,
April 10, 1864.

The Twelfth Corps has *officially* ceased to exist, and General Slocum has issued his farewell order, a copy of which I enclose.*

Last Thursday the officers of our regiment, accompanied by those stationed at this post, brought the band over and paid their respects to the General. Colonel Coggswell made a very good speech ; General Slocum tried to reply, but was so affected he could hardly speak, the tears running down his cheeks, but he finally managed to get through, and invited the officers to come in and spend the evening with him. There was plenty inside to eat and drink, and with the playing of the band and singing by a choir of officers of our regiment, a very pleasant evening was spent. The General was very much pleased with the whole affair, and will carry with him some very pleasant associations connected with our regiment.

I think I was mistaken, when writing my last letter, about the extent of the command at Vicksburg. From what I have heard since, I judge that it is quite an important district, though it may not be considered as important a command as a corps.

Well, the old institutions are broken up, and we must bear it as philosophically as possible.

* * *

---

* The Eleventh and Twelfth Corps were consolidated into the Twentieth Corps, under command of General Hooker.

FOUR MILES S. W RINGGOLD, GA.,
May 6. 1864.

An opportunity offers to write and send a letter, and I avail myself of it.

We left Tullahoma on the 28th of April, and, after a series of hard marches, arrived here last night, having come about a hundred miles. If I had time, I would write particulars of this trip, as it was, in some respects, a very interesting one.

We are now in position about five miles from Tunnel Hill, our corps forming the right flank of the army. In front of and extending along our line is Taylor's Ridge, where we picket. Sherman is evidently concentrating a very large force here. The troops from Knoxville are at Ringgold, and McPherson is moving Logan's Corps somewhere off on our right.

We all have perfect confidence that, if we can get at these beggars over there, we can give them an awful thrashing; but the question is, will they wait for our attack? I believe, though, it is Sherman's plan to follow them up very rapidly, as transportation for everything except rations is reduced to the minimum.

CASSVILLE, GA., May 20, 1864.

I take this, my first opportunity since the fight of the 15th, to let you know that I am alive and well. I will tell you briefly what we have done since my last letter was written from near Ringgold.

May 7th, we marched about seven miles to Trickam P O., taking up our position in line opposite Buzzard's Roost, which the enemy held in force. On the 8th and 9th we lay quietly in bivouac.

About seven A. M., on the 10th, we were moved off by a circuitous route to the southwest, passing through Snake Creek Gap in the afternoon, and camping at its outlet in the rear of McPherson's force. During May 12th the whole army, with the exception of the Fourth Corps and Stoneman's cavalry, concentrated in our vicinity. On the 13th everything moved forward towards Resaca, going into position near the enemy, and endeavors were made to bring on a general engagement; nothing more than skirmishing resulted, however.

On the 14th, fighting began early and lasted throughout the day: late in the afternoon we moved to the extreme left, where Howard (who had come down from Dalton) had been heavily engaged and worsted. We double-quicked into line, and opened on the rebels as they were advancing with a yell to take a battery from which they had driven our men; our fire checked them, then drove them back, and we advanced with a cheer, regaining all the lost ground. By the time we had done this, it was eight o'clock and bright moonlight, so our line was halted and strengthened during the night by a strong line of works. Early next morning, our regiment was selected to make a reconnoisance in our front to discover the position of the enemy. This was a very delicate manœuvre, but was capitally executed by Colonel Coggswell with the loss of only two men; the regiment behaved perfectly, not firing a shot, though under quite a disagreeable fire from skirmishers.

We developed the enemy's line and then returned, having done exactly what we were ordered to do. Soon after our return, our whole corps (now about twenty-two thousand strong), was massed for a tremendous attack on the enemy's right. At one P M., we moved rapidly forward and became at once engaged: our regiment was in the front line, supported on the left by the Twenty-seventh Indiana and on the right by the Third Wisconsin. We advanced about a half mile and then were stopped by a line of breastworks. Our skirmishers crawled to within a hundred yards of them, and our line formed close in the rear. We were hardly settled in position when the enemy massed quite a body of troops in our immediate front and advanced to the attack, with the evident intention of turning our left, which had become somewhat exposed; our regiment and the Twenty-seventh Indiana marched forward and met them with a cheer half way, and poured a terrible fire into their ranks, following it up with the " Virginia " style of shooting. The enemy seemed perfectly astonished, and fired wild and high; in less than half an hour, we had fairly whipped, with our two regiments, a rebel brigade of five regiments, killing and capturing large numbers of them ; our right and left did equally well. Night came on and the fighting ceased. The next morning, on advancing, we found no enemy. Since then, by a series of marches, we have reached this place. Yesterday, we came up with the enemy and had a very lively skirmish ; they left during the night. To-day we have been resting. The news from Virginia is grand, but the details terrible. So far, our losses in the regiment have been about thirty killed and wounded, no officers hurt. This is written in haste and with very little idea when it can be mailed.

May 22, 1864.

I open my letter again as an opportunity now offers of sending it quite direct. To-day the term of service of the old men of the regiment expires, and they start for Chattanooga to be mustered out; the Colonel and several other officers go with them to sign the necessary papers. Colonel Coggswell has just received an order to go to Massachusetts to expedite the forwarding of recruits to the regiment: he will give you the latest intelligence about me. You see by this, that for the present, I shall have command of the veterans, — not many of them, but men who can fight their weight, and a little more, anywhere.

To-morrow, in the words of Sherman's general order, we start on another "grand forward movement," with rations and forage for twenty days. Atlanta is evidently our destination: whether we shall reach it or not remains to be seen. One thing we are certain of — Johnston cannot stop us with his army; we can whip that wherever we can get at it. I wish the Army of the Potomac had no greater obstacle. We are now in a decidedly warm climate; the weather averages as warm as ours in July and August; what it will be when these months come, we can only imagine. I am, as usual, enjoying perfectly good health, and shall stand this campaign as I have all my others.

It is very painful to read the losses of friends in Virginia, — Stevenson, Abbott, and others. Here, outside of our own divisions, we know scarcely any one.

*   *   *

KINGSTON, GA., May 31, 1864.

My last letter was written from Cassville, and sent by Colonel Coggswell. On the 23rd the whole army made a movement forward, and successfully crossed the Etowah River by various bridges, camping on the south bank. The next day the Altoona mountains were reached and crossed, no great opposition being made except by cavalry. On the 25th the army moved, by several roads, towards Dallas, and skirmishing began. Suddenly an order came to halt, face about, recross the creek, and move to the left to support Geary. As I was crossing the bridge, an order came to me saying that the Second Massachusetts had been especially detailed by General Hooker to remain on that road and hold the bridge on which we had crossed.

About five P M., I heard our division "go in" about three miles on my left with a tremendous crash of musketry and artillery; the fighting seemed to last an hour, then suddenly stopped. The next morning I heard about our division's fight.

As soon as they arrived on the ground, they were formed in three lines, and made an impetuous attack on the enemy for nearly a mile into a strong line of works. Then Sherman found that he had the whole of Johnston's army in his front: he therefore immediately began concentrating his army, which was accomplished during the day of the 26th. McPherson, driving the enemy out of Dallas, formed in front of that place. His army constituted the right wing, Thomas the centre, and Schofield the left. Our division suffered severely in the fight, losing about a thousand killed and wounded, one-half being out of our brigade.

On the 29th I reported at headquarters. I found the division in reserve, a large part of it escorting trains to the rear.

♪ ♪ ♪

NEAR ACKWORTH'S STATION,

June 9, 1864.

My last was from Kingston : that place we left on the 4th, being part of a force to guard twelve hundred wagons to the front. Four days of hard work, night and day, carried us over the Altoona mountains to this place, where we joined the brigade.

We now occupy a very strong position, with the enemy in our immediate front. Their pickets and ours are on perfectly good terms : the men off duty meet each other between the lines, exchange papers, and barter sugar and coffee for tobacco. We shall probably make another grand movement in a day or two, which will carry us somewhere near Atlanta.

The loss in our corps so far has been about four thousand killed and wounded, — a heavier loss, I think, than any other corps has sustained in this army. We were about twenty-five thousand strong at the beginning of this campaign. Life is cheap this year almost everywhere in the army.

We don't indulge ourselves now in any irregularities of diet, but stick consistently to our pork and hard-tack moistened with coffee. Most of us probably eat about a third as much in weight as if we were at home doing nothing. Still, I have never felt in better health in my life, and feel strong and fit for work, notwithstanding the hot sun.

We are so far from home (that is, this army) that I don't think the newspapers pay much attention to what we are about, and seem to be conveying the idea that Johnston has only a small force, and is constantly reducing it to help Lee out of his scrape. I don't know how large an army is in our front, but I do know that wherever we bulge out, we find rebels who fire bullets fully as injurious to the health as any I have ever seen used. As yet we have had no great battles, but there has been a great deal of sharp fighting. I think Sherman means to get nearer Atlanta, and then have the grand smash-up.

✽ ✽ ✽

June 12. 1864.

I have another opportunity to write you a few lines. We have moved about a mile to the left and made a slight advance, and taken up a new position.

I would rather go into a pitched battle than be situated as we are now. Within five hundred yards of us is a rebel battery posted on a hill, which completely enfilades our line. We have thrown up heavy traverses, which I hope will protect the men, and I shall select a good tree for myself if there is any vigorous shelling. A little while ago they tossed a shell which killed one man and wounded another in the regiment on my left. This kind of a thing you expect in a battle, but when you are lying peaceably in camp it is rather disgusting.

How many more weeks this style of thing is going to last I can't tell, but I am sure that the majority of this corps is hoping for a general battle to end it.

✽ ✽ ✽

NEAR MARIETTA, GA., June 24, 1864.

My letter of the 19th brought our operations up to that date, and closed just as we were about to start on a fresh move. An advance of a few hundred yards brought us to their works, — a line so strong that if decently well held, I don't think it could be carried by assault by the best infantry in the world. We pushed on by the flank about a mile, then struck the enemy. All this movement was in a pouring rain (from the 1st to the 21st, inclusive, eighteen of the days were rainy), which finally came in such torrents that we were obliged to halt for two or three hours before making our dispositions.

The enemy was found entrenched on a ridge in our front. We began, just before night, to throw up a slight line of works to protect us from sharpshooters. I had the extreme right of the division. One of our men, First Sergeant Lord, of Company K, was mortally wounded while constructing breastworks ; he was a splendid fellow, and had been recommended for a commission.

At five o'clock on the 20th, our division was relieved by Wood's Division, Fourth Corps. We moved gradually along the line to the right, connecting at night with the left of the Twenty-third Corps : this gained us a position pretty well on the enemy's left flank. On the 21st our line was slightly changed ; on the 22d, our corps swung forward on its left in a north-easterly direction, the Twenty-third Corps following our movement, except that its right was well refused. The object of the movement was to take possession of the Powder Spring road, an important highway leading from Marietta. By stretching out our division into a single line, and connecting some parts of it with a line of skirmishers, its right just reached this road, and connected with the left of the Twenty-third Corps.

Before the troops were all in line, word was sent in from the skirmishers that the enemy was massing for an attack on our centre and left. We were just ready and nothing to spare, when Hood's Corps came out of the woods in our front (to my left, the length of about two regiments), and advanced, with their usual yell, in four lines. The division opened upon them with musketry and artillery, and before their first line had gotten within fifty yards, they were all broken and repulsed ; their loss was very heavy, as they were in entirely open ground. I think three or four hundred will cover our division's loss. I had only two men wounded. Towards the close of the attack our situation was very critical ; our ammunition was nearly exhausted, and not a single support was near. If there had only been one line behind us, we could have advanced at once and taken large numbers of prisoners. As soon as support did arrive, we advanced our skirmish line, but the enemy had gone, leaving their dead and hundreds of small-arms on the ground. I enclose you a fragment of the Fifty-third Virginia's flag, which was captured by the Fifth Connecticut.

I think our division has a right to brag a little on this fight, for if a single regiment had misbehaved, our line would have been broken. We are still in the same position as on the 21st, but there is a constant movement of troops to our right, threatening, you see, all their lines of communications and retreat. They still hold Kenesaw Mountain, which is due north from here. If they can only be forced to attack us, I think we can use them up completely. On the 21st, we took prisoners from three divisions, comprising the whole of Hood's Corps, which forms at least one quarter of their entire army.

I will give the Western army credit for their superior use of artillery. Wherever infantry goes, the batteries follow right in line, and in this way guns can be used continually at very short range, producing, of course, deadly effect. At Gettysburg, every colonel in our brigade besought the chief of artillery to put some guns in position in our line, but we were told that it couldn't be done, as the gunners would be picked off by sharpshooters. Here they have to take the same chances as an infantry man.

⚜ ⚜ ⚜

NEAR VINING'S STATION, GA.,
July 9, 1864.

The 2d of July, Saturday, I was Field Officer of the day, and had charge of the brigade picket. That night I received notice that the enemy were expected to leave very soon, and to watch them closely. I went out to the picket line, intending to stay there till morning: the night was pretty dark, and though only about three hundred yards of open field lay between our line and the rebels', yet nothing could be seen at that distance. Occasionally, shots were fired. At one in the morning I ordered three men and a corporal, whom I knew to be cool, brave men, to crawl up within a few yards of the nearest rebel picket post, if possible, and see if they were still there. In about an hour they returned, and reported that they had been near enough to hear the enemy talking, and had been fired upon twice; however, from general appearances, I made up my mind that they were going. and so reported.

At a little before daylight, the whole picket line was ordered forward. We advanced and got into the enemy's works without opposition, taking quite a number of prisoners. These works were the most formidable I have yet seen, — more of the nature of permanent fortifications than ordinary field works. The breastworks were of the strongest kind; then about ten yards in front was a *chevaux de frise* of a double row of pointed rails, and in front of this, an almost impenetrable abattis about one hundred yards wide.

I got into Marietta among the first with my skirmishers. I found it to be a beautiful place, though now almost deserted by its inhabitants. We drove out the rear guard of cavalry and artillery; among them could be seen numbers of citizens, men and women, running off like fools, leaving their property to be destroyed. For the first time in the South, I saw here pretty, neat country places, like those of Jamaica Plain and Brookline, with green lawns and hedges, and ornamental shrubs and trees about them; the houses appeared to be well furnished, but I suppose before this, the riff-raff of the army has rifled them of all worth taking. The Military Academy was a fine building, with gymnasium, etc., about it: it has been converted into a hospital. By sunrise the whole army was moving and on the heels of Johnston. We were right on him when he got into another of his lines of works. My skirmishers took about fifty prisoners; judging from that, the army must have taken at least one or two thousand.

July 4th, nothing occurred except a few changes of position. On the morning of the 5th, the enemy were gone from our front; we followed them up, and found them in their next line, about three miles off.

From one part of our line I had a distant view of Atlanta, the spires and towers rising in plain sight above the everlasting forests, which seemed to extend without a break, excepting an occasional corn-field, from Tullahoma to this place. We are now in front of the rebel position, their two flanks resting on the Chattahoochie, as do ours. We are told that we shall be here a few days, so I suppose there can be no obstacle to the enemy crossing the river whenever they want to do so. In my limited sphere of observation, I can give you for facts only what I see; the causes are all beyond me, as I know nothing of any movements beyond our own corps.

✌ ✌ ✌

NEAR VINING'S STATION, GA.,
July 15, 1864.

We are now enjoying a short respite from our exertions, which is very welcome after the campaign's hard work. By a series of movements and operations we have pushed the enemy south of the Chattahoochie, they now picketing their side of the river and we ours. It is difficult to tell anything about the result of this campaign, since, from appearances, the rebels are preparing to evacuate Atlanta with no more of a struggle than they made at Marietta, so that the fall of the former place is already calculated on as the result of the next move forward. The trouble is that we cannot get at Johnston and his army; he is too weak to meet us in a fair fight; his game, therefore, is to have a succession of lines of works prepared for him in his rear by citizens and negroes, which cannot be taken by direct assaults, but out of which, with our superior numbers, we can finally turn him. Whether we can follow an enemy of this kind farther than Atlanta, is a question in my mind, for we have already had to guard a railroad for over two hundred and fifty miles through a country swarming with guerrillas and roving cavalry. Johnston will undoubtedly retreat towards Macon, which will virtually abandon to us the whole of Alabama and Western Georgia, and cause the fall of Mobile.

There is an amount of cunning in this continual retreating of Johnston which is not generally allowed him. To be sure, he gives up a great deal of valuable territory, but he keeps his army intact and finally removes it out of our reach, leaving us an immense distance from our base, subject to raids on our line of communication and consequent stoppage of supplies; and supposing him at Macon, he is nearer to Lee, and can sooner transmit and receive reinforcements. This is the unfavorable side; but, on the other hand, the constant retreats of Johnston have, to a certain extent, demoralized the troops belonging in Kentucky, Tennessee, Northern Georgia and Alabama, so that on each occasion of their falling back, hundreds of deserters are brought into our lines; they all say that half the army would do the same if it dared, but they are told fearful stories of our treatment of prisoners and are also closely watched, and, when caught, shot without mercy. The case has occurred, repeatedly, of deserters lying all day in ditches and behind stumps, between our picket lines, afraid to stir from fear of being shot by their own men; as soon as night would come, they would come in. Without a single exception, I have seen these men always kindly and hospitably received by our soldiers; it is always,

" How are you, Johnny? we're glad to see you ; sit down and have some coffee, and tell us the news."

The amicable feeling existing between the men of the two armies when not actually fighting is very curious, and between the best troops on each side the understanding seems the most perfect. It is a proverbial expression, now, with the rebels, that Hooker's men are the toughest to fight, but the best to picket against. We have one rule now in our division, which entirely prevents all picket firing except in case of an advance of the enemy. Last Sunday I was Field Officer of the day and had charge of the brigade picket ; one portion of my line relieved a part of the Fourteenth Corps. When I first posted my men, it was necessary to crawl from one post to another and keep entirely out of sight, for before we came there had been a continual popping. In a short time it was discovered who had arrived, and all firing upon us ceased. The next morning, in broad daylight, I pushed my line down to the bank of the river without receiving a single shot, and afterwards rode along where the day before it would have been sure death or a disabling wound. We never yet have been the victims of any treachery, but, on the contrary, have received warnings in time to look out for ourselves. They will call out, " Look out, Yanks, we've been ordered to fire," and plenty of time will be given to get behind our works. When we fight, we fight to crush the rebellion and break the power of the rebel armies, not against these men as individuals ; there is no enmity felt, yet no one can complain of a want of earnestness or desire on our part for victory.

No news which has come to us for a long time has been received with such pleasure as that of the sinking of the Alabama by the Kearsarge. It is a great naval triumph for us, not over rebels merely, but over a Johnny Bull ship manned by English sailors, armed by English guns, fired by English gunners. It was an affair with England all through, and only needed, at the wind-up, to have that fair-minded, non-interfering Englishman carry off Captain Semmes, who had already surrendered, under a recognized British flag. Perhaps we cannot do anything now to help ourselves, but the time will come when we will make that mean, bullying English nation repent of her action towards us in this war; I hope I may live to see the day and help to wipe off these old scores. How long could she hold a foot square of territory on this continent against the immense armies we could raise, and what harm could she do us? We may not have as good a navy to-day, but we would have, and our coast would swarm with privateers.

War is a terrible thing, but a man should feel as jealous of the honor of his country and flag as he would of his own, and should resent an insult to the one as readily as he would to the other.

⁂

NEAR VINING STATION, GA.,
July 16, 1864.

The President, in his wisdom or his weakness, has stopped all capital punishment in the army. The greatest penalty for the crime of desertion now is confinement during the war at the Dry Tortugas: that may be for a longer or shorter period than the term of their enlistment, but during the whole time the deserters are not under fire, their hard labor is probably less than that which troops in the field have to perform, and the chance of escape is always before them. Is it humanity for a man virtually to pardon all these deserters, who have committed one of the greatest military crimes, when, by so doing, the life of every soldier who does his duty and goes into battle is endangered to a greater extent? I do not say that shooting deserters would stop all desertion, but I believe that with such a penalty before them, only the most reckless would attempt it. These men who desert are of no value to society, and no one would regret them if they were justly shot.

This war is now in its fourth year; no one doubts that it has got to go on in some shape or other, either well or poorly managed, till it is brought to a definite conclusion; that end may be in one year and it may be in five years, but should not there be some regard to economy in its conduct? Should it be possible for ten out of every fifteen thousand men, raised at an expense of four or five hundred dollars apiece, to escape their term of service due the Government? Why, at every little scare, are we raising hundred-day men and telling them, as a strong inducement to serve, that they will be exempt from any drafts during that period? A man cannot become a soldier in a hundred days; he can't learn in that time how to take care of his health and rations. The shorter the term of service the greater will be the proportion of deaths. No man in this war can look ahead for one hundred days and calculate on any great and decided success within that time. The chances are that at the end of that term, the occasion for men will be as great as at the beginning.

These calls for men for short terms are farces which have been repeated too often. They are made as concessions to a people who would as cheerfully stand a practical order for men. In the case of these bounty-jumpers, substitutes, and all other unreliable men, there should be an order obliging them to deposit their bounties in some bank, payable only by small instalments, or at the end of their term of service. A man furnishing a substitute should be held responsible for him during the whole three years. I am willing and have made up my mind to serve through this war, no matter how long it lasts, with pay or without pay; and I do want to see a little more practical earnestness in the conduct of affairs, and not so much shirking of responsibility.

✻ ✻ ✻

IN THE TRENCHES,
ONE AND A HALF MILES FROM ATLANTA,
July 25, 1864.

Considerable has been accomplished since my last. On the 17th, I was on picket on the north bank of the Chattahoochie; late in the afternoon I was ordered to withdraw my line, as the army was moving to cross the river a few miles above. As my sentinels left, over the river bank, the rebels called out, "Have you got marching orders, Yanks? We are off at six." I joined the brigade about ten that night, crossing on pontoons.

The next day, we marched to Peach Tree Creek, about four and a half miles from Atlanta, our second division securing a crossing. On the 20th, all of Thomas's army was over and in position fronting Atlanta. McPherson and Schofield, with the Fifteenth, Sixteenth, Seventeenth and Twenty-third Corps, by a flank movement, had crossed the Charleston Railroad and pushed up quite near Atlanta; about noon, our pickets and theirs connected. We were busily at work strengthening our position, when, without a word of preparation, the rebels in heavy force burst upon our picket line. Our brigade was in the second line. The first line advanced and breasted the shock in fine style. The fighting was quite severe till dark, when the enemy were repulsed and retired to their works. Our corps lost sixteen hundred killed and wounded, and buried five hundred and eighty-one rebels in front of its line. The loss in the regiment was trifling, — Captain Sawyer severely wounded and three men not severely. Skirmishing continued throughout the 21st.

On the 22d the enemy retreated to their main line of works around Atlanta ; we are now encircling them closely. The Macon Railroad is still in possession of the rebels, but it is the only one left to them. Operations now bear the character of a siege ; there is constant cannonading going on from each side night and day, and consequently we have to stay in the trenches all the time. A few minutes ago a shell burst in the Third Wisconsin on our left, severely wounding three officers who were together in a tent. Just above us is a twenty-pound Parrott battery, which has fired, with hardly an intermission, for forty-eight hours ; every shell is supposed to drop in the city. Since we have been here, there have been three or four assaults on our line, but they have all been repulsed without difficulty. We are now strong enough to resist anything.

I was told the following story, which was brought in by a citizen who lives in the outskirts of the city, in a fine house in plain sight of our line. He says that a few days before our arrival here, Davis, Johnston, Bragg, and other officers met at his house for consultation. After considerable talk, Davis expressed himself very much dissatisfied with Johnston for his constant retreats. Johnston said he had done what, in his opinion, was for the best; that he had brought off his army intact, but that he had not felt strong enough, at any time, to offer or accept battles ; in conclusion, he said that if the President thought there was any officer who could manage his army better than he could, he would at once tender his resignation. Upon this, Johnston was relieved and the command offered to Hardee ; he declined the honor, saying that he had perfect confidence in Johnston, and if, in his (Johnston's) opinion, Atlanta couldn't be held, he was bound to agree with him. The army was then offered to Hood, who jumped at it and said he would have Sherman on his way north in twenty-four hours. Hood believes in fighting, and has probably lost ten thousand men since he assumed command ; but, as yet, we continue to look towards the Gulf.

NEAR ATLANTA, July 31, 1864.

The evening of the 29th, I went on duty as Field Officer of the day of this brigade. After posting my picket and seeing that all was right, I lay down to take a little sleep.

I must now explain our position. The right of our brigade rests on the Chattanooga Railroad and connects with the left of the Fourteenth Corps ; the picket line was about one hundred and fifty yards in advance of the line of works. The rebel rifle pits extended along a crest about two hundred and fifty yards in front of their works, which consist of strong redoubts connected by a heavy line of breastworks ; at a point about in front of the centre of my picket, the ridge rose into a prominent mound. It was swept by the guns of two forts and several batteries, and appeared to be untenable even if taken.

About half-past two A. M., on the 30th, I received an order to advance and take the rifle pits in my front, if possible, and then hold the position. I was told that the pickets on my right and left would advance with me and protect my flanks. My picket consisted of one hundred and sixty-one men and five officers. At a given signal, just at dawn, the whole line rose up and moved out of their little works; for fifty yards not a shot was fired, then the enemy discovered us and opened their fire. I gave the order, "Double-quick," and in a moment we were upon them: in less than two minutes we had captured seventy-two prisoners, including four captains and three lieutenants. I caught one fellow by the collar as he was making off; he seemed almost frightened to death. Says he, "Don't kill me,—I surrender, I surrender." I told him that I wouldn't kill him, but he must tell me truly if there was anything between the pits and the works. He said no, but that there were lots of men and guns in the works. On my left, the picket had come up well, refusing its left so as to connect with our old line. On my right, as I soon learned, the Fourteenth Corps picket, seeing that we were being peppered a good deal, thought they would stay where they were, so I had to bend my right away round to cover my flank. The mound was now ours; the question was, could we hold it? The instant that we were fully in possession, I set to work fortifying. The men were in high spirits, knowing that they had done a big thing, and I felt confident that they would fight well. In a very few minutes we had rails piled along our whole front, and bayonets and various other articles were in requisition for entrenching tools.

As soon as the rebels were fully aware of our proximity, and just as it was becoming fairly daylight, they opened on us along our front with musketry and artillery, throwing enough bullets, cannister and shell for a whole corps instead of an insignificant picket detail.

Work, of course, was now suspended. Our greatest annoyance was the fort, which mounted heavy guns, and these were so near that they seemed almost to blaze in our faces and were doing a great deal of damage. I ordered part of the men to fire into the embrasures. In less than five minutes, heavy doors were swung across the openings, and the fort closed up business for the day; the other batteries were out of sight, and kept up their fire. After about an hour of this kind of work, I found that I had lost a good many men, and the others were much exhausted. I sent off an orderly with the report that I must have reinforcements, if I was expected to hold my position. Word came back that I should have more men, and that General Thomas said that the position must be held. Shortly after, three companies reported to me, and about six A. M., the old "Second" came up.

All the men who could be spared from their muskets were kept at work digging, so that every minute we were becoming stronger, and the danger was growing less; still the artillery fire was terrible. At ten o'clock, Colonel Coggswell sent in word that his men could stand it no longer; they had fired over a hundred rounds of cartridges apiece; they were perfectly exhausted and must be relieved. The Thirteenth New Jersey came out and the Second went in; this regiment was under command of a captain, so that it came under my control. At eleven the fire began to decrease, and from then till two P M., as the rebels found we were to hold on, it continued to subside. A little after two, an officer was sent out to relieve me. My loss was forty-nine killed and wounded, at least half having been hit by solid shot and shell.

I had a whole chapter of wonderful escapes. One shell burst within ten feet of me, throwing me flat by its concussion and covering me with dirt. As I was trying to eat a little breakfast, a rifle bullet struck the board on which was my plate, and sent things flying; but it seemed that my time to be hit had not come.

Our regiment lost three killed and seven wounded. George Thompson was slightly wounded by a piece of shell, nothing serious. The recruits behaved well, without exception.

The best news we have is that General Slocum is coming back to this corps.

* * *

NEAR ATLANTA, August 8, 1864.

We have not yet quite reached our goal, though the prize seems almost within our grasp; movements are constantly being made to invest the city more closely, and we must soon take it. The rebels are making a very obstinate defence, and have works which can never be taken by assault. Several attempts, thus far futile, have been made to cut the Macon Railroad: when we succeed in that, the enemy must leave. The length and severity of this campaign is beginning to tell on almost everybody. You can judge somewhat how it is; for three months, officers and men have been on active duty, and, during that whole time, they have lived on the never-changing diet of pork, hard bread and coffee, with occasional fresh beef; every one looks thin and worn down; large numbers of sick are sent to the rear every day.

Hardly a day passes without one or more casualties : one day last week we had three men wounded in camp, two by bullets, one mortal, and one by shell. I was standing in front of my tent watching their shells burst, when I saw one come through a tree in front, strike the ground and ricochet. I knew by its direction that it must come into camp, and followed it with my eyes. It was a twenty-pounder with a disagreeable whiz and end-over-end motion and it went into a squad of three men, breaking the thigh of one of them. He bore it very quietly, had the bone set, and was taken off to the field hospital on a stretcher.

✤   ✤   ✤

Near Railroad Bridge, Chattahoochie,
August 30, 1864.

We have changed our base, as you may perceive. On the night of the 25th, we learned that our corps was to go back to the river and hold a strong " *tête du pont*," covering the bridges and ferries, while the remainder of the army made a grand movement towards the right to get position on the Macon Railroad. Our move was executed very well, all the caissons and wagons going to the rear on the night of the 25th, the troops remaining in position during the next day and moving back at night.

Our division holds a very strong line, covering the railroad bridge and two important wooden ones for wagons. We have made ourselves very strong here, with good earthworks and timber slashed into an impenetrable abattis for five hundred yards in our front, and are now ready for any part of the rebel army that sees fit to attack us. Hood will probably have all he wants on his hands, to look after Sherman and his communications. The 27th was a bright day in our calendar. On that day, General Slocum returned and took command; he rode along our position, and was received with the greatest enthusiasm by the whole line. I had a chance to shake hands with him and say a few words. He is looking finely. I set him down now as one of the very best generals in the whole army, and I think time will prove him so. He is, in every way, a good soldier, and what is better, a true man, devoid of humbug and "rich in saving common sense." Professional bummers and loafers must make themselves scarce now, and men who do their duty will be recognized once more.

*   *   *

ATLANTA, GA., September 6, 1864.

I take my first opportunity to write you a few words. Our corps came in here on the 2d and took possession. Colonel Coggswell was put in command of the post by General Slocum, with two regiments besides his own for guard. I was appointed Provost Marshal of the city, and have been overrun with business ever since. I have an office in the City Hall and quarters in an elegant house near by. Our corps and the Fourteenth are to occupy the defences of the city. General Slocum commanding. You can imagine my hands are full of work, being "Mayor" and answerer of all questions to the citizens of a good-sized city, besides having to look after cotton, tobacco, and other valuable stores, and arrest all marauders. However, I have got the thing in run-

ning order now, and, with my two assistants and their clerks,
shall get along very well.

We shall be here a month or two, probably. Sherman and
Thomas will make their headquarters here in a few days.

⁂ ⁂ ⁂

ATLANTA, GA., September 11, 1864.

To-day being Sunday, my office is closed, and I have a
little time to tell you of some of the events of the last
ten days.

September 2d, about eleven o'clock, we received the glorious news that Atlanta had been surrendered to a reconnoitering party from our Third Division. Our First Brigade
was immediately sent forward to occupy the place, and about
four P M., the whole corps followed. We entered the city
about dark, with bands playing, etc. Our regiment went into
camp in the City Hall Park, having been detailed as the provost guard. The next morning, we took possession of the
City Hall. I took the court-room for my office; the other
rooms were taken for headquarters, guard-rooms, etc. My
private room was with the Colonel, in one of the finest houses
of the city, opposite our camp, — Brussells carpet, elegant
beds and other furniture. The family were very glad to have
us occupy the house for their own protection; they are very
fine people, and I think have very little sympathy with the
South.

Our first few days were terribly hard ones, but now that
the army is settled in position and we have reduced things to
a system, we are getting along very well; I doubt if to-day
there are many cities in the North, of the same size, which

are quieter or cleaner than this one. Atlanta is a very pretty place, and less Southern in its appearance than any I have seen. It is quite a new town, and its buildings are generally in good condition; there are, on the principal streets, some fine warehouses, banks and public buildings; the depots are the best I ever saw for railroad accommodations. There are large numbers of elegant residences, showing evidence of a refined population; in a good many cases they are deserted. Our shells destroyed a great deal of property, but I am sorry now that a single one was thrown into the city, for I don't think they hastened the surrender by a day. They did not harm the rebel army, the only casualties being twenty harmless old men, women and children, and two soldiers. There are differences of opinion about this kind of warfare, but I don't like it. General Sherman is going to make this a strictly military point, and has ordered all citizens, North or South, to remove within a limited time; the present population is ten or twelve thousand, so you see it is no small undertaking.

This measure, although it seems almost inhuman, I believe to be an actual military necessity; it is simply one of the horrors of war. We shall send people North who have always lived in a state of luxurious independence, but who will arrive there without a dollar of our money; their only property being their household furniture, etc. The gentleman who owns this house, a Mr. Solomon, is a fine old man; he is seventy-two years old and in poor health. It is a most pitiable sight to see him walking about his house and grounds, bent over with age and suffering, and to think that he must leave his home where he has lived so long. Fortunately, he has a son-in-law in Nashville, who is well off and will take care of him; but,

as he says, it is pretty hard for a man of his years, who has
been independent all his life, to have to depend on charity
now.   He had a son, a classmate of General Howard's, who
died in the United States service about five years ago.

This is only one of hundreds of cases, but thinking or feeling about them is useless.   I shall do what I can to get them
off comfortably.   There is a sort of armistice here for ten
days.   Trains of the two armies will meet at a fixed point and
transfer their passengers and goods.

Sherman says that we shall wait here till about the end of
October, when the corn crop will be ripe, and then go down
and gather it.   He is the most original character and greatest
genius there is in the country, in my opinion.

*   *   *

ATLANTA, GA., September 13, 1864.

The families are fast moving South ; a large wagon train
goes out each day, conveying them to General Hood's lines.
The family in whose house our rooms are, is going North ; I
wish they were going to stay, so that we might continue to
enjoy the nice beds and furniture.   However, we shall have
our balcony left, on which we spend our evenings.   It is quite
a place of resort for the staff officers and others in town
who call on us, especially as our brigade band, or the Thirty-
third Massachusetts', plays in front of the house almost every
night.   I enclose some pieces of a rebel flag which was
captured here and presented to me ; they will answer as a
memento of our entrance into the city.   General Sherman
told an officer of our corps that the reason he left the Twentieth Corps behind was because he knew he was going to

take Atlanta by this last movement, and he wanted the corps which had done the hardest fighting and the hardest work of the campaign to have the honor of entering the city first; I believe this is honest, for there is very little humbug about General Sherman.

*   *

ATLANTA, GA., September 18, 1864.

Yours of the 9th was received to-day. Since my last letter, I have kept pretty busy with the affairs of the post, but nothing new or startling has occurred in my line of duty. Our corps, with the Fourth and the Fourteenth, occupy the works near the city. Howard with the Fifteenth, Sixteenth and Seventeenth, is at East Point, and Schofield with the grand Army of the Ohio, is at Decatur. Troops are in comfortable quarters and leaves of absence and furloughs are being liberally granted. There is just now a ten days' truce for sending families South and the exchange of prisoners.

Before the Chicago Convention. I told you my opinion of McClellan. I am willing to acknowledge that I have changed it greatly since his letter of acceptance. His letter, as you say, was patriotic, and would have suited me if it had refused the nomination; but when he closed by saying that he thought his views expressed those of the Convention, he changed, in my opinion, from being an honest, straightforward soldier, into a politician seeking office.

He knew, as well as we know, that a large part of the Convention was for peace and not for war carried on in any way, and as an honest man he had no business to say what he did. It has always been the boast of the Democratic party that whoever their candidate might be, he had to carry out the principles of the men who elected him. The peace men must have shown their hands plainly, and whatever McClellan may say now to disown their support, they will have a baneful influence upon him, if he is elected.

Colonel Coggswell is commanding this post in a manner which reflects great credit upon him; he stands high with Generals Thomas and Slocum; even Sherman has complimented him, and spoken of the appearance of our regiment. He is, I think, one of the best practical soldiers I know; his chances for promotion are very good; I hope, for the sake of the service, his and my own, that he may get it.

It is altogether a good thing for us that we are here in the city; as I said before, it is all owing to General Slocum. His firm and just rule is felt already throughout the corps; men who have shirked, and, to use an expressive word, "bummed" all through the campaign, are getting snubbed now, while those who have done their duty quietly and faithfully are being noticed.

Sherman is an entirely different style of man. He is a genius and a remarkable one, and is undoubtedly the longest headed, most persistent man, not even excepting Grant, there is in this country, but he is too great a man to be able to go into details. He cares nothing, apparently, for the discipline and military appearance of his troops, or at any rate, leaves that for his subordinates to see to; he cares nothing, either, for doing things through regular channels, but will give his orders helter-skelter, any how; this, of course, is an eccentricity of genius, but it is a very troublesome one at times.

✳   ✳   ✳

ATLANTA, GA., September 25, 1864.

It would surprise you, or any one else outside of the army, to see what an important military post Atlanta has already become ; the storehouses in the vicinity of the depots are piled full of commissary, quartermaster and ordnance stores, and, even now, we are thirty days ahead on rations; the tracks are crowded with cars and engines, and to all appearances, there is as much going on in the centre of the city as in the busiest parts of New York or Boston. Most of the families have moved out, though a number still remain, probably with the intention of staying until they are actually forced from the city. The family from our house left on Tuesday, for Nashville; I felt quite sorry to have them go; they made very pleasant society for us, and it seemed very much like home, living with them. We are now in entire possession of their house, and are living in state and style. The house is a new and very fine one, built of brick with stone trimmings, every part of it finished in good shape.

Isn't a soldier's life a queer one? One month ago, we were lying on the ground in a shelter tent, with nothing but pork and hard bread to eat; now we are in an elegant house, take our dinner at half-past five, and feel disposed to growl if we don't have a good soup and roast meat with dessert; after that, we smoke good cigars on the piazza and have a band play for us.

What a splendid victory was that of Sheridan's! I have never spoken of Dr. Heath's death; he is a great loss to us every way, — the best surgeon we ever had, and a pleasant, genial companion.

* * *

ATLANTA, GA., October 16, 1864.

On the 2d, Sherman started with most of the army in pursuit of Hood, leaving General Slocum with the Twentieth Corps and about twelve hundred other troops, to take care of Atlanta. Hood's movement is a desperate one, but we are not anxious as to the result of it; we have rations to stand it longer than he can; forage is the only question, and that we are getting in considerable quantities from the country. If the enemy had obtained possession of Altoona Pass, we should probably have been obliged to evacuate.

Our latest news is that Sherman is at Resaca and Hood on the road near Dalton. We have received a few glorious despatches from Grant, and are most anxious to hear the result of his last movement. This post has been and is being most effectually fortified. The old rebel works bear no comparison to ours; with our corps, we could easily stand a siege by Hood's whole army.

The present campaign out here affords ample chance for speculation. I have not yet seen a man rash enough to try to explain Hood's intentions, or how he feeds his army. One thing is certain: if Sherman gets a fair chance at him so far away from his base, with no line of communications to fall back upon, he will smash him. We shall know very little of the political campaign this year, but we shall probably survive that.

Poor Dr. Heath! He was one of the best men I ever knew, — a pleasant, genial, kind-hearted companion, and as good a surgeon as I have ever seen in the army; his loss has been felt throughout the whole division. He fairly wore himself out in the service; this whole summer he has been surgeon of our division hospital and principal operator, in which position he worked himself to death. I hope we may get a good man in Heath's place. Crowninshield and Storrow will probably arrive here by the first through train.

ATLANTA, GA., October 26, 1864.

Yesterday, Captain Crowninshield and Mr. Storrow arrived, after a long journey of thirty days. I think Storrow will prove a good officer; I like his looks very much.

We are still occupying our mansion, quietly living on the fat of the land. Every other day, a forage train of seven or eight hundred wagons goes out about twenty miles into the country, and comes back the third or fourth day loaded with corn, sweet potatoes, flour, chickens, etc. Yesterday, our small mess wagon brought in two barrels of flour, two or three sacks of sweet potatoes, a dozen chickens and ducks, a jar of honey, a keg of sorghum, and several other small articles; so you see that we are not likely to starve for some time to come.

General Sherman says that, as the Georgians have seen fit to get in our rear and break our railroad, we must live on Georgia. Of course, very heavy guards have to go with these trains, for the country is full of cavalry; thus far, however, they have all returned safely.

We keep a cow in our back garden, and have cream in our coffee and new butter every day; we also keep ducks and pigeons. In the city there are concerts or negro minstrel entertainments every night; the concerts by the Thirty-third Massachusetts Band are very good indeed.

ATLANTA, GA., Nov. 3, 1864.

I am now going to let you into some of our mighty secrets, which, probably, when you receive this, will be no secrets at all.

We are going to abandon Atlanta, first utterly destroying every railroad building, store, and everything else that can be of any use to the rebels. The railroad from here as far north as Resaca will be entirely destroyed. Then, cutting loose from everything and everybody, Sherman is going to launch his army into Georgia.

We shall probably march in two or three columns to Savannah, destroying all railroads and government property at Macon and Augusta, and taking up all rails on our line of march. Isn't the idea of this campaign perfectly fascinating? We shall have only to "bust" through Joe Brown's militia and the cavalry, to take any of these inland cities. Of course, the taking of Savannah is only the preface to taking Charleston. Colonel Coggswell, with five regiments, has been ordered to prepare this place for destruction; he has given me the charge of about half of it. I have just submitted my proposition how to do it.

The proposed movement is the most perfectly concealed I have ever known one to be; scarcely an officer on the staff or anywhere else knows our destination or intention. There are all kinds of rumors which are told as facts, but they only more effectually conceal the real campaign. We shall be lost to the world for a month or six weeks; then shall suddenly emerge at some seaport, covered with dirt and glory. I like the idea of a water-base amazingly; no tearing up railroads in our rear, no firing into trains, and no running off the track.

General Thomas will be left, with fifty thousand or sixty
thousand men, to guard the line of the Tennessee. I suppose Hood will bother him considerably, but that is none of
our business. If Hood chases us, we can whip him as we
have done before, and we have the best of him in the way of
supplies, as we shall eat up ahead of him. I feel perfectly
confident of success, no matter what course the rebels take.
General Slocum will have command of the two largest and
best corps in the army, and will show himself the able man
he is. Sherman will have a chance to compare him with his
other army commanders.

✿ ✿ ✿

ARGYLE ISLAND, GA.,
December 18, 1864.

An opportunity offers to send a few lines home. We are
now on an island in the Savannah river, very near the Carolina shore, our principal duty being to guard a rice mill which
is threshing out rice for the army. A gunboat and shore
battery have tried to drive us off, but we still hold our own.
To-day we shall probably receive rations from the fleet; for
the last week, the army has been living entirely on rice and
some fresh beef. No operations as yet are going on against
the doomed Savannah. I imagine that Sherman is waiting
for a force to come through from Port Royal and connect
with our left, so as to invest the city thoroughly, and cut off
all retreat for the enemy. As soon as we get settled anywhere, I will write an account of our last campaign, though I
can't do it justice in any letter. Such a variety of experiences as we have passed through during the last forty days,
I never dreamed of.

We had a very jolly Thanksgiving, although we marched that day from Milledgeville to Hebron, fifteen miles. Turkeys and sweet potatoes, honey and various other luxuries, were served at our table at eight P M., and we drank to the memory of the day in some old apple-jack of the country.

❧ ❧ ❧

NEAR SAVANNAH, GA.,
December 24, 1864.

Our campaign has been successfully ended, and we are again in camp preparing for a few weeks' rest and comfort. Since my note to E——, we have had the hardest time of the whole campaign since leaving Atlanta. On the 15th, about two P M., our regiment was ordered to the river; on arriving there, we were shipped on flat boats and crossed to Argyle Island, with considerable difficulty, getting aground once, and being shelled at long range by a rebel gunboat. We camped that night with the Third Wisconsin on a rice plantation. The object of our move was to protect a rice mill which was threshing out rice for the army, and to prepare a crossing into South Carolina. The remainder of our brigade crossed to the island on the 16th. That same morning, our threshing operations were suddenly brought to a standstill by a rebel battery, which opened on us from the South Carolina shore; this caused the most amusing skedaddle of about a hundred negro operatives, men, women and children, that I ever saw.

We got two guns into position and silenced the rebs. On the 19th, after several delays, our regiment, the Third Wisconsin, and the Thirteenth New Jersey, started at daylight, and, under cover of a heavy fog, crossed to the South Carolina side, effecting a landing without loss. We advanced at once, driving in about a brigade of rebel cavalry. After having secured all the desirable positions, we entrenched ourselves, and received the support of the remainder of our brigade and two guns. The enemy were much annoyed by our movement, and in the afternoon made quite a decided attack, charging in one place almost up to the works.

Our position was a peculiar one. With our five regiments, we held a line about two and a half miles long. The whole country is a rice swamp, divided into regular squares by dykes and ditches, with occasional mounds raised a few feet above the water level. On a series of these mounds our regiments were placed, connected along the dykes by a thin line of skirmishers. Our ground being perfectly open and level for miles, we could see every manœuvre of the enemy.

On the 20th, the enemy pressed as close to our lines as they dared, showing a very superior force to our own, and in the afternoon opened a battery in our front, and fired from a gunboat in our rear, in a manner which was by no means comfortable. Early in the morning of the 21st, news came of the surrender of Savannah, and orders for our immediate crossing into Georgia. Most of our regiments and the two guns were transferred to Argyle Island, when the enemy began to advance rapidly into our old position; they were easily checked, but with them in our front and a gale blowing on the river, it became a very difficult and dangerous operation to cross. However, by ten P M., that night, the last man was on the island, though he had to swim the river.

Now I must go back to about four P M., that same day, when our regiment attempted to cross to the Georgia shore. Arrived at the landing, no boats capable of carrying anybody were to be found. Captain Grafton and I took a light "dug-out" and went across to send some over. Two "flats" were found and sent back, and the regiment put on them. The largest of the two, containing the majority of the men, had, with great difficulty, struggled against the wind and tide and nearly reached the shore, when an irresistible gust struck it, turning it round and round, and sending the poor boat up the river towards South Carolina with great speed. Grafton and I pursued them in our light boat, and found them about seven P M., hard and fast on the lee shore of Hutchison Island, whence, after a deal of work, they were ferried back, a few at a time, to Argyle Island.

Such a row back against the wind as we had is easier imagined than described; however, at twelve at night, we were safe on Georgia soil with a fraction of the regiment. The next day was spent mainly in ferrying the brigade over. Towards night we started for camp, and reached it after a hard march of nine miles. This expedition cost us a few very good men wounded, but no officers.

I haven't as yet heard any estimate of the guns, stores, etc., captured, but I understand that everything was left behind. The city has been well protected since our occupation; the citizens seem very well contented that it has changed hands, and show themselves freely on the streets. We are camped about two miles from the city; the river is not a stone's throw from my tent. We are collecting quite a fleet of light boats, so that we shall have plenty of opportunity for rowing. Our next move will probably be to take Charleston.

❧ ❧ ❧

Near Savannah, January 2, 1865.

Without going much into detail, I will give you a general idea of our last campaign as we saw it. The minor experiences I shall leave till I come home some time, to amuse you with.

The 15th of November, the whole corps left Atlanta at seven A. M.: previous to that time all heavy buildings had been battered down with rails, tracks torn up, etc., so that everything was ready for the torch. The Fourteenth Corps and our post command was not to move until the 16th. As soon as the city was pretty clear of trains the fires were set. It is impossible for you to imagine, or for me to describe, the magnificent spectacle which this city in flames presented, especially after dark. We sat up on top of our house for hours watching it. For miles around, the country was as light as day. The business portion of Atlanta, embracing perhaps twenty acres, covered with large storehouses and public buildings, situated in the highest part of the city, was all on fire at one time, the flames shooting up for hundreds of feet into the air. In one of the depots was a quantity of old rebel shells and other ammunition; the constant explosion of these heightened the effect. Coming from the sublime to the ridiculous, in the midst of this grand display the Thirty-third Massachusetts band went up and serenaded General Sherman; it was like fiddling over the burning of Rome! While the conflagration was going on, we kept large patrols out to protect the dwellings and other private property of the few citizens remaining in the city; this was effectually done.

On the morning of the 16th, nothing was left of Atlanta except its churches, the City Hall and private dwellings. You could hardly find a vestige of the splendid railroad depots, warehouses, etc. It was melancholy, but it was war prosecuted in deadly earnest. The last of the Fourteenth Corps did not get off till about half-past four P M. We followed after, being the last United States troops to leave Atlanta. That night we marched eleven miles, going into camp four miles beyond Decatur.

From this time until the 22d, we marched as rear guard of the Fourteenth Corps, crossing the Yellow, Alcofauhachee and Little Rivers, passing through Conyers, Covington and Shadyvale, and arriving at Eatonton Factory on the 21st. Here we left the Fourteenth Corps and followed the track of the Twentieth, which was on the road leading from Madison through Eatonton to Milledgeville.

On the 22d, we passed through Eatonton, and came up with the rear of the Twentieth Corps at Little River, which we crossed on pontoons.

On the 23d, we marched into Milledgeville, joining our division across the Oconee River. The capital of Georgia is a very one-horse place, with a few good public buildings including the Capitol, which is quite handsome. Here, for the first time since leaving Atlanta, we got into camp before dark, and therefore had a little rest, which was much needed. We had averaged getting up at half-past four A. M., and into camp at eight P M., which, with an intermediate march of fifteen miles, made a pretty good day's work. Two hours are none too many to allow for getting supper and pitching shelters.

At six A. M., on the 24th, we were off again; it being Thanksgiving day, our excellent cook had provided us with a cold roast turkey for lunch at our noon halt, and at night, after getting into camp near Hebron, he served us with turkeys and chickens, sweet potatoes and honey, in a style which did honor to his New England bringing up.

The 25th, we crossed Buffalo Creek, after some delay, the bridge having been destroyed by Wheeler's cavalry, which skirmished with our advance.

On the 26th, Wheeler had the impudence to try and stop our corps. Our brigade, being in advance, was deployed against him. We drove them on almost a double-quick march for six miles into the town of Sandersville; the Fourteenth Corps' advance, coming in from the north, struck their flank and they scattered, leaving their killed and wounded in the streets. Our whole loss was not more than six. That night we struck the railroad at Tennill; we destroyed several miles of it before going into camp.

The 27th, we marched to Davisboro, a pretty little place, rich in sweet potatoes and forage for our animals.

The 28th and 29th, our division destroyed the railroad from Davisboro to Ogeechee River. The army way of "repairing" railroads is this: the regiments of a brigade are scattered along for a mile, arms are stacked, and the men "fall in" on one side of the track. At a given signal, they take hold of the rail, tie, or whatever is in front of them; the order, "Heave," is then given, which means lift, and lift together; at this, the whole length of railroad begins to move, and the movement is kept up until the whole thing goes over with a smash. The ties are then collected and piled up; across each pile three or four rails are laid; the whole is then set on fire; the heat makes the rails red hot in the middle, and their own weight then bends them almost double. In many cases each rail was twisted besides being bent.

November 30th, we crossed the Ogeechee.

December 1st and 2d, we were rear guard ; the roads were bad, and we didn't get into camp before eleven or twelve P M.

December 3rd, we halted within a quarter of a mile of the pen where our prisoners were kept, near Millen. I rode over and looked at it. No description I have ever seen was bad enough for the reality. Situated in the centre of a moist, dismal swamp, without a tree inside the stockade for shelter : you can imagine what the place must have been in this climate in August. There wasn't a sign of a tent in the whole enclosure ; nothing but holes dug in the ground and built up with sod, for our men to live in. Eight bodies, un-buried, were found in these huts ; they were of men probably too sick to be moved, who were left to die alone and uncared for. Every one who visited this place came away with a feeling of hardness toward the Southern Confederacy he had never felt before.

The marches of the 4th, 5th, 6th and 7th brought us to Springfield, twenty-seven miles from Savannah. The country is generally poor and swampy, the roads bad. On the 8th, the corps trains were left in the rear, guarded by the Third Division, the First and Second going along unencumbered. We had to cut our way through the trees which were felled across the road by the rebels.

On the 9th, we encountered a redoubt on the road, fifteen miles from Savannah ; this was soon carried with a small loss, our brigade flanking the position.

On the 10th, the army formed line of battle for the first time since leaving Atlanta, six miles from Savannah, fronting the rebel works. The rest of the story you know. Altogether, the campaign was brilliant and successful ; in many respects it was a fatiguing one, but to make up for the hard work the men generally had an abundant supply of sweet potatoes, fresh beef and pork. Since the 10th, and up to the present time, rations for men and officers have been very short, but they are now improving.

We are threatened with another campaign immediately; I imagine it will be a move towards Columbia, threatening Augusta and Charleston.

There was no mistake made in the amount of force left with Thomas, as the result has shown. The rebellion has one front only now, — that is in Virginia, and we are going to break that in before next summer.

Savannah is a very pretty, old-fashioned city, regularly laid out, with handsome houses, etc. The officers on duty here are having fine times, even better than ours at Atlanta. Sherman reviewed the whole army, a corps at a time, last week. Considering the ragged and barefooted state of the men, they looked well.

⁂ ⁂ ⁂

HEADQUARTERS SECOND MASS. INF'Y,
NEAR SAVANNAH, January 8, 1865.

We are liable to move very soon; rations are coming up pretty fast, and clothing has been issued to most of the army. Everyone anticipates hard fighting before we strike another base; it seems most probable that Lee will come out of Richmond and give us a fight before he will allow us to take up a position immediately threatening his communications.

⁂ ⁂ ⁂

HEADQUARTERS SECOND MASS. INF'Y,

SAVANNAH, GA., January 15, 1865.

Our latest and most important item of news is Colonel
Coggswell's promotion to the position of Brevet Brigadier.
I think it is a well deserved promotion; he has always commanded his regiment well, and I feel confident he will do
himself credit with a brigade; at any rate, I am glad to continue to serve under him, for he is to have this brigade. This
promotion, of course, puts me permanently in command of
the regiment, although at present the Colonelcy will not be
vacated; but I believe it will be long before the regiment
will have men enough to muster me. It is rather discouraging to sign a morning report showing an aggregate present
of only two hundred and fifty men, and for duty only one
hundred and ninety. I have applied to the War Department
for the detail of an officer for recruiting, but with our past
experience as a guide, there is very little to hope for, even
if that is granted.

Sherman's last general order to his army was a capital
one; it told every man what this campaign had accomplished,
and was written in his *piquant* style. Sherman is giving
great attention to the careful shipment of the cotton seized
here; every bale is weighed and numbered, and marked
U. S.; there is the usual number of agents, etc., trying to
get their hands on it, but I think there is a fair chance that
this lot will go straight to the Government.

We should have started on the march before this if we
had not had to wait for supplies; as yet, there is no accumula-
tion of rations here, but they are expected daily.

If you can help me in any way towards getting recruits,
please do so.

HEADQUARTERS SECOND MASS. INF'Y,
SAVANNAH, GA., January 16th, 1865.

This afternoon, orders came quite unexpectedly for us to be ready to move to-morrow morning at seven o'clock. Our corps, I believe, crosses the river and marches up to Sister's Ferry, where the Fourteenth joins us from the south side; after that, it is a mere speculation where we may go. I am inclined to believe that the railroads towards Columbia will receive our attention, so that communication between Richmond, Charleston and Augusta may be cut off.

General Coggswell has been assigned to duty according to his rank, by the President, and takes command of the Third Brigade, Third Division, of this corps, — not our brigade, as I expected. He published a very good order, taking leave of the regiment, and left, taking with him, I believe, the good wishes of all.

To-day I sent a request to the War Department for six hundred conscripts; whether it will effect anything or not, remains to be seen. I think they ought to be willing to fill up the oldest regiment in the volunteer service of the country.

Every one anticipates hard fighting on this campaign, and I don't think we shall be disappointed; if we are successful, Richmond is on its last legs.

      ✻ ✻ ✻

HEADQUARTERS SECOND MASS. INF'Y,
PURYSBURG, S. C., January 25, 1865.

On the 17th, we broke camp, and after some delay crossed the Savannah River (i. e., our division), and marched about eight miles into South Carolina, camping at night in the old camps of the Third Division. The next day we marched at twelve, noon, and accomplished seven miles more. The 19th, we started at nine A. M., marched through Hardeeville, and camped at Purysburg, on the river. The march was over a very bad road, overflowing in some places to a depth of two feet. About noon, the rain began to fall in torrents, and it became evident, even then, that forward movements would be suspended for a time. Late in the afternoon the gunboat Pontiac came up the river, convoying the transport R. E. Lee (late rebel), loaded with rations.

The 20th, 21st, 22d and 23d, it rained almost incessantly, flooding the whole country about us, so that it was possible almost to row a boat over the road we had marched, back to Savannah. The corduroying was washed away, and the pontoon bridge broken; part of our train was cut off and had to return to Savannah. Of course all movement was stopped, and we set to work to make ourselves as comfortable as possible. By a system of very extensive ditchings, I managed to get the camp on comparatively dry ground. We had quite easy communication with our base by the river, so that supplies were received without difficulty.

Yesterday I rode back to Hardeeville and called on General Coggswell. I found him very pleasantly situated. He has a good staff. I believe that, if he has time and opportunity, he will have the best brigade in this army; his faculty for commanding is very great, and he is interested in his work.

I am very much in hopes that my application for conscripts will do some good. I put it pretty strong, and I think got a good endorsement from General Slocum, and I hope from Sherman. The fact that we have never yet received a single drafted man under any call, ought to go a great ways; the oldness of the organization, its small numbers, and its being the only veteran Massachusetts regiment in Sherman's army, ought to do the rest. I am glad to see that the Provost Marshal General has ordered that no recruits be received for any but infantry commands. With all these things in my favor I shall expect to receive, at the end of this campaign, at least eight hundred good men, all of the best moral character and warranted not to desert for at least three days after assignment.

What a delightful proof of Butler's unfitness for command was General Terry's gallant and successful assault of Fort Fisher. Grant's letter transmitting the official reports was one of the best snubs I ever read.

*   *

HEADQUARTERS SECOND MASS. INF'Y,
ROBERTSVILLE, S. C., January 31, 1865.

Since my last letter we have pushed farther into this miserable, rebellious State of South Carolina. We came very slowly, as we had to cut our way for the first ten miles through continuous rebel obstructions; but after that distance, the enemy evidently began to think it was no use trying to stop us, and the fallen trees became fewer and further apart. As we marched on from Purysburg, we gradually got out of the swamps and into rich plantations showing signs of the wealth of their old owners. Just think of single fields comprising at least one thousand acres. In the centre or in some part of each one of these great fields, would stand the universal cotton press and cotton gin. The planters' houses were rather better than the average through Georgia, but none of them were what we should call more than second or third class houses in the North ; generally they stand half a mile or a mile back from the road, at the end of a perfectly straight, narrow avenue, in fact, nothing more than a cart path.

The most of them are surrounded by magnificent old live oaks and cypress trees, draped all over with the gray Spanish moss which gives to the deserted mansions a very sombre, funereal appearance. In rear of the houses are the rows of negro quarters, and the various outbuildings required on large plantations. So far, on this march, I have seen only one white male inhabitant and very few negroes. Every place is deserted ; the valuables and most of the provisions are carried off ; but I went into one house where there were rooms full of fine furniture, a fine piano, marble-topped tables, etc.; there was a valuable library in one room, of four or five thousand volumes. I saw a well bound copy of Motley's Dutch Republic, and a good set of Carlyle's works. This property is, of course, so much stuff strewn along the wayside. Unless there happens to be a halt near by, no one is allowed to leave the column to take anything ; but stragglers, wagon-train men, and the various odds and ends that always accompany an army on the march, pick up whatever they want or think they want, and scatter about and destroy the rest, and by the time the last of a column five or six miles long gets by, the house is entirely gutted ; in nine cases out of ten, before night all that is left to show where the rich, aristocratic, chivalrous, slave-holding South Carolinian lived, is a heap of smoldering ashes.

On principle, of course, such a system of loose destruction is all wrong and demoralizing; but, as I said before, it is never done openly by the soldiers, for every decent officer will take care that none of his men leave the ranks on a march. But there is no precedent which requires guards to be placed over abandoned property in an enemy's country. Sooner or later, of course, as we advanced and occupied all of the country, it would be taken, and I would rather see it burned than to have it seized and sent North by any of the sharks who follow in the rear of a conquering army. Pity for these inhabitants, I have none. In the first place, they are rebels, and I am almost prepared to agree with Sherman that a rebel has no rights, not even the right to live except by our permission.

They have rebelled against a Government they never once felt; they lived down here like so many lords and princes; each planter was at the head of a little aristocracy in which hardly a law touched him. This didn't content these people; they wanted "their rights," and now they are getting them. After long deliberation, they plunged into a war in order to gratify their aristocratic aspirations for a Government of their own, and to indulge in their insane hatred for us Yankee mud-sills. The days of the rebellion are coming to an end very fast; even its lying press cannot keep up its courage much longer. For a year they have met with a series of reverses sufficient to break the spirit of the proudest nation, and this next spring will see a combination of movements which must destroy their only remaining bulwark, Lee's army, and then the bubble will burst; and I believe that we shall find that Jeff Davis and other leading Confederates will be abused and hated by men of their own section of country more than they will by the Northerners.

No, I might pity individual cases brought before me, but I believe that this terrible example is needed in this country, as a warning to those men in all time to come who may cherish rebellious thoughts; I believe it is necessary in order to show the strength of this Government and thoroughly to subdue these people. I would rather campaign it until I am fifty years old than to make any terms with rebels while they bear arms. We can conquer a peace, and it is our duty to do it.

This little, deserted town of Robertville we reached two days ago; our whole left wing is close by. We shall fill up again with supplies, and in about two days strike into the country. Barnwell, Branchville, Augusta, Columbia, and Charleston are all threatened. I hope the rebels know as little as we do which one is in the most immediate danger of a visit. Wheeler's cavalry is all around us, but as yet no infantry. A regiment of his command tried to stop our coming into this town. The Third Wisconsin, without firing a shot, charged them, broke them all to pieces, and lost only three men.

CAMP NEAR FAYETTEVILLE, N. C.,
March 12, 1865.

An hour ago, we were all astounded by the announcement that a mail would leave headquarters at four P M. If you had quietly stepped up to my shelter and asked me to come and take a comfortable Sunday dinner at home, I should have hardly been more astonished. It seems that there is a steam tug up from Wilmington, and that we have captured two steamers at this city. I write now only to say that I am perfectly well, and have been in but one skirmish since leaving Savannah. When I have time, I will give you a history of this campaign; all I will say of it now is that it has been a hard one. We have had a great many severe storms; the roads have been awful, and the obstacles in the shape of rivers, streams, and swamps, most numerous; but we have conquered them as we have everything else.

When I tell you that since the eighth day of February I have not drawn from the commissariat a single government ration, you can understand how entirely we have lived on the country. There have been times of great anxiety, when it seemed as if the country could yield nothing, but we have always had great herds of cattle to fall back on, so that there was never much danger of suffering. This has been no picnic excursion, I can assure you, and I am not sorry we are nearing a base. Another Sunday will, I hope, see us in Goldsborough. I hope to get some express matter soon, as I am in sad condition in the way of clothing.

We have marched from Cheraw since last Tuesday morning, about seventy miles.

[The writer was wounded at the battle of Averysboro, March 16, and went to Massachusetts, where he remained about sixty days.]

❧ ❧ ❧

HEADQUARTERS SECOND MASS. INF'Y,
NEAR ALEXANDRIA, May 23, 1865.

I have been sorely exercised for the last few days on account of learning, when I joined my command, that I had been mustered out of service by order of the War Department, on account of being absent from the effects of wounds received in action.* Yesterday, through the kindness of General Slocum, I obtained an interview with General Townsend, Adjutant General, and presented to him an application for the rescinding of the order; it had received pretty heavy endorsements from all my superiors, and was at once granted. The veteran regiments are probably to be retained, for the present at any rate; they will be filled up to the maximum by consolidation.

Everybody is scrubbing up for the review to-morrow, which will be a great affair. I am sorry you are not coming on. I am getting along very well with my wound.

☞ ☞ ☞

HEADQUARTERS SECOND MASS. INF'Y,
NEAR WASHINGTON, D. C., May 26, 1865.

We are now settled in what we suppose will be our permanent camp for quite a long time. It is a lovely place about four miles from Washington, and very near Bladensburg.

The regiments are scattered so that each has plenty of room. Day before yesterday was the grand review. We started from our camp between five and six A. M., reached Capitol Hill about eleven, and soon after started down the avenue. I had as prominent a place for the regiment as I could ask for, on the right of the brigade. The regiment looked finely, and was cheered and applauded by name sev-

---

* Immediately after the surrender of Lee's and Johnston's army, the War Department issued a General Order honorably discharging every officer then absent from his command on account of wounds or sickness.

eral times. The day was a very fatiguing one, but one which will never be forgotten by any of us. After passing the reviewing officers, we marched about six miles to our present camp; it is a very pleasant exchange from the Virginia side of the Potomac.

HEADQUARTERS SECOND MASS. INF'Y,
June 10, 1865.

Our old corps, division and brigade, have been broken up, and yesterday we marched out of our beautiful camp and away from every old association. The Third Wisconsin cheered us and we cheered them, but a good many of us felt more like blubbering. Our division is composed of the veteran regiments of the Twentieth Corps belonging in the Eastern States.

WASHINGTON, D. C., June 18, 1865.

Since my last letter we have made one more change, and the regiment now forms part of the garrison of Washington. That we have been detailed for provost duty in this city shows that though we are now among strangers, we are not altogether unknown.

We are camped quite near the Capitol, in a not very aristocratic neighborhood. We have considerable guard and patrol duty to do, now that so many troops are passing through on their way home.

WASHINGTON, D. C., July 8, 1865.

I suppose you have seen the announcement before this that we are to be mustered out of the service at once. We shall probably be home in a week or ten days ; how long we shall be delayed there, I can't tell.

You may not hear from me again till I get home.

[The regiment was mustered out of the service at Readville, Mass.. July 26, 1865. The total losses of the regiment in killed and wounded during its entire term of service were: 14 officers and 176 enlisted men killed or mortally wounded, and 26 officers and 410 enlisted men wounded, not mortally. Total casualties in action, 626. Died of disease, 84 ; drowned, 4.]

APPENDIX.

THE "VETERAN" FURLOUGH.

THE regiment received its orders to go home for its thirty days' furlough January 9, 1864, those who had not re-enlisted remaining in camp at Tullahoma, Tenn. Movements by rail were slow in those days, owing to insufficient transportation, and it was not until the evening of January 18th that the regiment reached Boston. There was a great throng at the Boston and Albany station awaiting it, but no formal reception was given that evening. The men were marched to barracks on Beach Street, and quartered there for the night; the officers were entertained by Mr. E. R. Mudge at the United States Hotel, and many of them went to their homes for the night.

The next day, January 20th, was a fine, bright, winter day, not too cold for comfort. At about 9 A. M., the regiment filed out of the Beach Street barracks, and, under the escort of the Boston Cadets, began its march. It was an ovation from the start. The men had spent much of their time the preceding night in polishing their brasses and belts, and brushing up their well worn uniforms. Their rifles and bayonets were burnished to the last degree, and would have passed the inspection of the most rigid West point martinet. It is difficult to say too much in praise of the appearance of the command on this occasion. The men were veterans in the truest sense, and their whole appearance indicated it. Their march was the easy swing of the old soldier, but in perfect time and alignment, with every face set squarely to the front. Their faces, bronzed by exposure to the sun and the weather, had the expression of hardihood which only comes to men accustomed to meet dangers and privation. The officers were all young men, hardly one who marched that day being more than twenty-five years old, yet from the military point of view they were entitled to be called veterans. Colonel Coggswell, who commanded the regiment, was then in his twenty-fifth year; Captain Crowninshield, who had been three times wounded, was in his twenty-first year and was the youngest captain, but several other officers of this rank were only a year or two older.

The march was first through the West End of Boston, passing through Arlington Street to Beacon Street, — the reception proper really beginning on the latter street. The sidewalks were filled with a cheering multitude, and every window and balcony were crowded with friends, who gave the most enthusiastic greeting to the regiment as it passed. It was a stirring march, to fine martial music, and no one who marched with the regiment that day will ever forget this thrilling episode of his military life.

From Beacon Street the march proceeded through the business streets, where the principal stores had been closed by common consent. On State Street was another ovation from "the solid men of Boston," who filled the street and cheered most enthusiastically as the column marched by. When Faneuil Hall was reached the men filed in, and every inch of available room was immediately filled by the crowds which followed. The galleries were occupied by ladies and many of the immediate friends of the officers and men. The hall was handsomely decorated by flags and streamers, with the State arms and shield on each side of the clock.

The officers and color guard with their shot-riddled battle flag were on the platform, where Governor Andrew and his staff, Mayor Lincoln, General Burnside, and other distinguished men were assembled. Mayor Lincoln presided on the occasion, and after prayer by the Rev. Dr. Lothrop, a collation was served to the men. Mayor Lincoln then made an address of welcome, which he closed by introducing "His Excellency the Governor, who, in behalf of our honored Commonwealth, will formally tender you that welcome which your merits and patriotic services deserve."

Governor Andrew followed with an eloquent address, in which he recounted the services of the regiment and followed its career through its various campaigns. He referred by name to many of those who had fallen in battle, and told the story of the color bearers who fell one after another at Gettysburg, but who never let the flag touch the ground, in a manner which thrilled every one who heard him. In conclusion he said: "Now, Mr. Commander and soldiers of the Second, I have not attempted by words to declare how deep is the gratitude of the Massachusetts heart towards the living, — how sacred our remembrance for the memory of the dead. Brave and true men lean not on the speech, rely not on the assurance of the lips. Soldiers, you know that from the bottom of her heart Massachusetts admires, reveres and loves you all."

Colonel Coggswell made a modest, well-spoken reply to Governor Andrew's speech of welcome, and was followed by General Burnside, who happened to be present in Boston at that time, and who made a few remarks suitable to the occasion.

After the exercises at Faneuil Hall were concluded, the regiment marched to Coolidge Block, Court Street, where the arms and equipments were deposited, and the men received their thirty days' furlough.

The officers scattered to their homes to enjoy this brief season of rest, although an active effort was made to secure recruits to take back into the field. This effort entirely failed, mainly owing to the unfortunate policy, then in effect, of creating and filling up new military organizations, rather than placing every recruit in the old regiments or other organized commands.

On Monday, February 22, the regiment assembled at Beach Street barracks, and the next day, at half-past four P. M., left Boston for Tennessee. An entire week was spent on the return trip, and the regiment finally reached its camp at Tullahoma on a dark, rainy morning, where it rejoined the comrades who had been left behind.

THE BATTLE OF AVERYSBORO.

MARCH 15, 1865, the day preceding this battle, was cloudy and rainy, the brigade marching about ten miles on a plank road, getting into camp after dark. The camp was in an ancient grave-yard, very damp and disagreeable. Our men had just started fires and were preparing their frugal supper, when a mounted orderly clattered up to my shelter tent with orders for the regiment to be ready to march at once. Our brigade was soon in motion through the pitchy darkness, over the most execrable of mud roads. We marched only about five miles, but it was nearly twelve o'clock when we filed off the road into a pine thicket, and lay down on the wet ground for the remainder of the night. During the night march we learned that Kilpatrick's cavalry had encountered a force of the enemy, and that we had been ordered up to relieve one of his brigades. This force was General Hardee's command, which had been halted in a strong position for the purpose of holding Sherman's advance, to give time for Johnson to concentrate his army at some point beyond. About seven A. M., I received orders to form the regiment on the left of the brigade, throw out skirmishers and engage the enemy, and was told that my left would be supported by cavalry. The ground in our front, over which we advanced during the day, was a pine swamp, the water in some places being a foot or more in depth.

As soon as the regiment had taken its position, I ordered Captain J. I. Grafton, who commanded the left flank company, to take his company and the one next on his right, and deploy them in front of the regiment. The skirmishers were at once engaged, and we came under a well-directed, scattering fire. Captain Grafton was just placing his men in position when he was wounded in the leg and started to the rear, but when within a few yards of the place where I was standing he turned again to the front, and almost immediately was struck by a bullet in the neck. Even with this mortal wound he staggered several paces to the rear, when he fell, and died a few moments afterwards. Captain Grafton was a gallant soldier, and a gentleman in every sense of the word. He joined the regiment as junior second lieutenant in November, 1861. He was severely wounded at Cedar Mountain, and again at Chancellorsville. The latter wound was in one of his legs, which caused a lameness from which he never fully recovered, but in spite of pain and discomfort he maintained his place at the head of his company at all times, and with his fine bearing was an example of a gallant soldier. It seemed hard that he should meet his death after passing through the great campaigns of the war, and when the regiment was in action for the last time; but so it was, and we had to mourn the death of one more brave and true comrade.

The skirmishers of our brigade steadily pushed back those of the enemy, and after our ammunition was exhausted, we were relieved by General Coggswell's brigade of the Third Division, the remainder of the Twentieth Corps having now come up to the front and taken the place of the cavalry. Coggswell continued to press the enemy with his brigade, and advanced for about a mile until he encountered a line of breastworks into which the enemy had retreated. In the meantime our brigade, the Third of the First Division, had been transferred to the right, and late in the afternoon we were ordered forward again. Our last advance carried us close to the enemy's works, and we became hotly engaged. The action lasted until dark, when the firing subsided, and during the night the enemy retreated from our front.

The regiment carried into this action only 141 officers and men: the companies were mere skeletons. Captain Grafton, with two companies, had but twenty men under his command when he was killed. The casualties in the action were Captain Grafton and seven enlisted men killed or mortally wounded; Lieutenant-Colonel Morse and fourteen enlisted men wounded. Lieutenant Samuel Storrow, who had joined the regiment at Atlanta and had made the "March to the Sea," was detailed as aide on General Coggswell's staff when the latter was placed in command of a brigade at Savannah. Averysboro was his first real battle, and he went into it full of zeal and courage. While carrying an order he was struck by a bullet, and although the wound did not seem serious he could not rally from its effect, and died a few hours after. He was a fine, spirited young fellow, and his loss was greatly felt by those who had been associated with him during his short term of service.

The battle of Averysboro was a comparatively small affair, but the fighting was spirited, and the march of Sherman's army was but little delayed by Hardee's efforts.

The battle of Bentonville followed on March 19, but the Second Massachusetts Regiment was not actively engaged.

THE FINAL ORDER.

HEADQUARTERS SECOND MASS. INFANTRY,
WASHINGTON, D. C., July 12, 1865.

General Orders, No. 26.

To THE OFFICERS AND MEN OF THE SECOND MASSACHUSETTS INFANTRY : —

The Lieutenant-Colonel commanding takes this, his last, opportunity to tender to you his congratulations, that, after more than four years of hard service, you are enabled again to go to your homes, and resume your peaceful avocations.

A brief review of your history in this regiment cannot fail now to interest you.

At the very outbreak of the late rebellion, the Second Massachusetts Infantry was organized. Its first year of service was not an eventful one, and it became famous only for its good discipline and appearance.

In the campaign of 1862 it had a more distinguished part to act. On the night of May 24, your regiment, by its steadiness and bravery, beat back greatly superior forces of the enemy, and saved Banks' little army from total destruction. All of honor that can be associated with the disastrous retreat of the next day certainly belongs to you. Next came Cedar Mountain ; there, with the same determined bravery, this regiment faced and fought three times its numbers ; and, in twenty minutes, lost more than one-third of its enlisted men, and more than one-half its officers. Antietam, Chancellorsville, Beverly Ford, Gettysburg, and the great campaigns of the West, with their numerous battles and skirmishes, followed in quick succession ; and the war ended, leaving with you a most brilliant and satisfactory record, — a record of courage, gallantry, and tenacity in battle, of unflinching steadiness in defeat, of good discipline in camp, and of respect and prompt obedience to all superiors; this is the record which you can take to your homes, and it is known and acknowledged throughout the length and breadth of your State.

The Lieutenant-Colonel commanding does most sincerely congratulate you who are now left in this command, on having passed safely through this great struggle, which has terminated so gloriously. He feels sure that no one of you will ever regret your part in this war. As long as you live, and whatever your future in life may be, you will think of your soldier's career with the greatest pride and satisfaction; its hardships and sufferings, its dangers and glories, have made you all nobler, better, and more self-reliant men.

It will not be with pleasure alone, that you recall the events of the past four years. With sadness you will bring to mind the appearance of this regiment as it marched out of Camp Andrew, July 8. 1861; and will think how many of the noblest and best officers and men then comprising it now fill soldiers' graves. You will cherish the memories of these gallant men; and though you lament their loss, you will remember that they died in battle, bravely doing their duty, fighting for their country and right; and you will thank God, when you look about you, and see peace restored to this entire country, that the sacrifice of their lives has not been in vain.

The Lieutenant-Colonel commanding thanks you for your adherance to your duties, and your fidelity to him, since he has had the honor to command you. He assures you, that, in taking leave of this old organization, he feels more pain than pleasure; he has been with it since its first existence, has shared its dangers, privations, and glories; and now that it has devolved upon him to write these words of farewell he does so with unfeigned regret.

In conclusion, he hopes that the lessons taught by this war will exert a beneficial influence on your future lives, and that you may become good citizens and worthy members of society.

C. F. MORSE,
Lieut.-Col., Commanding Second Mass. Infantry.

(Official.)

www.ingramcontent.com/pod-product-compliance
Lightning Source LLC
Chambersburg PA
CBHW030120030726
47498CB00007B/2472